Eliza

and the

Raptor

t'Sade

Copyright © 2014, t'Sade

Curious Cabbit Press

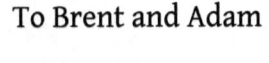
To Brent and Adam

Acknowledgements

My deepest thanks for my first-round victims, I mean readers: Shannon, J.T., M.B., and Brent.

And to those who help me turn it from an idle idea into something special: Ralph, my editor, and Mamabliss, who made the kick-ass cover.

Contents

Caught Red-Handed

Eliza closed her eyes as her Terick-class fighter accelerated out of the fighter bay of the FCM *Quantor*. The g-forces pinned her to her padded seat and crushed her armored flight suit against her body. With her eyes closed, she could almost imagine hands holding her instead of the uncaring might of physics.

"Third Lieutenant Midoze 73," came the impersonal voice of the fight controller. "It is a violation of launching protocol to limit any sensory input."

She opened her eyes and glared at the display in front of her. She knew the controller couldn't see her, but it didn't matter. Nothing she could say would ever disturb the AI. She spent many of her patrols day-dreaming of ripping the damn machine out of the server room and smashing it.

"One point has been deducted from your promotion."

Eliza flicked her gaze to the upper left of her ship's display as the AI helpfully displayed the points toward her next promotion: 17. A far shot from the 16,000 she needed, but two points shy of her peak that year. She rolled her eyes and leaned back to watch the lights flash past as her ship continued to accelerate out of the launch tunnel.

Seconds later, her ship rocketed out of the tunnel and into the darkness of space. The rumble of the jets shook the cockpit, and the pressure pinning her into her seat relaxed. She let out a soft gasp of breath and sank forward.

A holographic display bulged from her cockpit screen, expanding into a three-dimensional map of her surroundings. Unlike most displays, the center was not centered around her tiny fighter ship but the FCM *Quantor Generation Ship*, a hollowed-out asteroid end-lessly falling toward a ring of sixty-four microscopic singularities projected in front of it. Her computer display immediately marked out the extents of the event horizons, the point where her ship would be crushed in an instant.

The AI beeped once. "Third Lieutenant Midoze 73, for your 2,019th patrol, you are required to pass through the following way-points." Sixteen points appeared in a rough circle around the as-teroid. Each day, the points were randomly chosen and assigned. "Choose your starting waypoint and sequence."

It was the only choice the AI begrudgingly allowed Eliza: where to start the ten-hour flight and which direction to travel. She pointed to the nearest one and tilted the control rod to line up her ship.

"Reminder, there is a 0.627 probability for surprise during today's patrol."

Eliza scoffed. There was always chance that the tedious patrol would be interrupted with a surprise communication from her su-periors. It never happened in three years. No one cared about her, her patrol, or anything other than mindlessly doing the same damn thing every day.

The AI didn't respond. Instead, it started through the random-ized list of tips and notices before her route. "Reminder, removing your hand from your control stick for more than three seconds is a violation."

She squirmed at that one. Last week, she was trying to figure out some way of relieving the boredom of her flight when she lost another point. As she thought about how close she got to opening her flight suit to grope her nipple, she pressed her thighs together. The armored suit prevented any rubbing or friction, but the pressure against her sex gave a hint of pleasure.

"Warning, your pulse is increasing."

"Um," she cleared her throat. "Just getting excited about the pa-trol." Her soft, almost girlish voice, filled the cockpit.

"Your enthusiasm has been noted," came the impassive reply. "Reminder, waypoints must be flown in the order chosen. Any devi-ation is a two-point violation."

She fought the urge to scoff again. Instead, she pressed her thighs harder together and imagined her fingers caressing along her naked skin. It sparked little tingles along her nerves, and she could hear her breathing growing deeper and faster.

"Reminder, always be vigilant."

Struggling to hide her growing excitement, she glanced up at the controls and then down again. She tightened her hand into a fist before relaxing it. Two nights ago, she learned from an overheard conversation at dinner that the medical diagnostics disabled many of the pilot sensors while running, including the recordings of what she was doing. A bit of frantic research brought confirmation and a time. Twenty-one minutes to do whatever she wanted to her body, as long as she was suited and had her hand wrapped around the control stick when it ended.

Her nipples pebbled underneath her suit. The snug material prevented any rubbing, but she could feel the crinkling and the ache. She wished there was someone else in the cockpit with her, someone to fuck, or even just kiss in all the right places. She wondered what it would be like to be nipped.

She glanced up at the display and forced herself to calm down. She could wait a few more minutes for the AI to disconnect before risking everything for a stupid thrill. She knew she could have lost more points, but she didn't care anymore. She had to do something to break up her flight and the lure of violating every procedure she knew was too much. She needed it.

Her gloves creaked around the stick. She took a deep breath and another, trying not to think about the heat bubbling from between her legs, the ache of her nipples, or even the caress of her suit as her breathing crushed her breasts against the fabric.

"Reminder, lifting your feet for more than six seconds is a violation."

She couldn't wait to try, but she needed the AI's lecture to complete. She should wait longer, but her need beat against her senses. Everything in her life was boring and random. Her mission hours, random. Her waypoints, random. Her hours, just as mathematically random as everything else. Even the reminders were randomized, in theory to keep her from getting bored, but flight after flight simply pointed out the AI only had a few hundred to choose from.

"You may now proceed with your patrol. All serve the greater good."

Eliza muttered the required response. "The greater good."

The AI disconnected with a click.

She almost came at the sound alone. Her free hand slid along the rubberized keyboard but she held herself. Biting down on her lip, she stared at the menu key while keeping her ship aimed directly for the first waypoint. Her breathing echoed loudly in the ship, and she ached to rip open her flight suit and shove her hands between her thighs, but she held back.

Holding the control stick tightly, she aimed steadily for the first waypoint. She didn't want to wait but the growing anticipation added to her excitement. She only had twenty-one minutes and every second of holding back would simply add to the intensity. She used the time to think about everything she was going to do. Her imagination pushed her closer to the edge, and she distracted herself by rhythmically squeezing her thighs together until juices dribbled from her sex.

An hour later, she reached the first waypoint. It was just another point in space, but as her ship sailed through it, the computer chirped in confirmation, and the AI spoke up. "Notice, you have reached the waypoint three minutes, twelve seconds ahead of schedule. Slow down by 12.2% and continue to the second waypoint."

Eliza bit her lip as she panted. Her eyes focused on the link icon, waiting for the AI controller to disconnect. Her free hand hovered over the keyboard. Her fingertip caressed the rubberized menu button.

The microseconds stretched into infinity. The icon remained steadily glowing, and she feared that, somehow, the AI knew her plans.

The disconnect click shot out in the confines of her cockpit. A heartbeat later, the light darkened.

Eliza let out a soft gasp and slammed her finger down. Moving with imagined practice, she rapidly brought up the medical system and activated the diagnostics. There was no indication the cockpit sensors were disabled along with the network connection, but her impromptu research assured her she had her twenty-one minutes of freedom.

Releasing the control stick, she brought both hands to the keyboard and rapidly programmed the auto-pilot. It was a violation to use it for patrols, but she needed her hands free. As she programmed in the last direction, she pawed at her suit and fumbled with the clasp.

Ironically, the flight suit was not designed to be opened in flight. The rubberized fasteners resisted her fingers until she grabbed the opening with both hands and yanked it open.

Her breasts, small mounds tipped with aching nipples, crinkled in the cool air as she tore open her suit. She grabbed her right tit with her left hand and pinched her nipple. The sparks of pleasure that exploded along her senses brought a gasping moan to fill the cockpit.

Eliza arched her back and tugged at her suit. It resisted, but she pulled it open enough to slap one hand against her firm belly and jam it down underneath the armored fabric.

Panting, she strained to force her hand past the suit's resistance and along her sweat-slicked skin. Her pussy clenched with anticipation. Her moans became cries as she clawed for her pussy, fingernails slipping on skin until she caught the ridge of her pubic bone.

As soon as her fingertips ground against her clitoris, she freed her other hand and grabbed her breast again. Eyes closed, she arched her back from the padded chair and pumped her fingers into her soaked sex. Her labia clung to her fingers, despite the uncomfortable angle and confines, but every stroke sent tremors of pleasure coursing through her body.

"Fuck!" she cried out and arched her back, trying to somehow jam her hand deeper against her crotch. She lifted her foot from the cockpit floor and kicked the button to disable the controls. A moment later, she planted her heel on the keyboard and lifted her body higher to give her more access to her cunt. With every stroke, the sharp edge of an orgasm rose inside her.

She clawed at her breast, leaving shallow scratches across the smooth skin. The burn of her cuts added to her pleasure and she continued to rip at herself, crying out with every wet thrust into her aching pussy.

"Midoze!"

Eliza snapped open her eyes and let out a scream. On the display in front of her was Colonel Ritan 69, a dour man with a wrinkled face. Now, his glare had furrowed his brow until there was nothing but starkly shadowed lines on his face.

She threw herself back into her seat. "Fuck!"

A sharp pain radiated from her wrist as it tried to bend in the tight confines of her suit. She yanked at it, but couldn't free it from the pressure between her sweat-slicked body and her armor. Fumbling, she released her breast and brought it up into a salute, though with the wrong hand.

The colonel growled under his throat. "Do it properly, Third Lieutenant!"

Eliza's cheeks burned as she tugged at her wrist. Her fingers bumped against her pussy, the rush of her orgasm quickly dissipating. When she couldn't, she gave an apologetic look to the scowling colonel and pried open her suit with her free hand. She had to yank her hand free with a grunt.

Her nipples scraped against the fasteners of her suit as she brought her hand up to a salute. The ridge of her palm rested against the side of her temple. The smell of her pussy, tangy and sweet, flooded through the cockpit.

The colonel took a deep breath before he spoke in a deep growl. "You have failed your inspection."

She trembled; her mind and body struggled with her near orgasm and the terror of her seeing her colonel before her. On the side of her head, a rivulet of her juices ran down the side of her head. It was hot and slick.

She watched as the colonel's eyes flickered to the side and she held her breath. His gaze followed the dribble of juices running down the side of her face. Her entire universe focused on the sensation of the hot droplet tracing her chin and down her throat. It caught the swell of her breast before she couldn't feel it anymore.

"You are a disgrace to your ship," growled the colonel. "A disgrace to your uniform, and a complete disgrace to everything the

FCM stands for!"

Eliza winced at the booming voice filling the cockpit. From the corner of her eye, she saw the AI had boosted the volume for effect.

"Eyes forward!" snapped the colonel.

She sat up straight, shaking in fear. Her breasts hung out of her uniform. She could feel the fasteners of her suit scraping against her nipples with every gasping breath.

The colonel took a deep breath. "You are to finish your patrol. When you land, you better have a good explanation for... for..." His scowl somehow deepened. "This! And if you don't, you will spend the rest of your life in prison, or I will personally shove you out the damn airlock!"

The connection disconnected and her cockpit plunged into darkness. She exhaled with a sob, her body shaking violently.

As she fumbled to close her suit, she began to cry.

Dressing Down

Nine hours later, the tears had stopped, but Eliza still didn't have an explanation that could even remotely justify her actions. She doubted the colonel would believe she was simply bored of the endless patrols and needed an orgasm to pass the hours. Or to break the tedium of her life on the asteroid.

The FCM didn't approve of desire, sex being the top of a very long list of actions that were immoral in their eyes. The entire reason the FCM left civilization in a two-hundred generation trip to a distance star system was to flee sex, drugs, and deviant music. The generations born on the ship, such as Eliza's, didn't have that choice. They were FCM from the day they were cloned in test tubes.

As her ship approached the FCM *Quantor*, the computer chirped as it authenticated itself with the control systems and the computers took control. The tension in the flight stick went slack and she released it, just as protocol demanded. Unable to do anything, she rested her hands in her lap and waited.

The points toward her promotion had disappeared somewhere during her patrol. Now, there was nothing but a blank spot where the numbers used to be. She dreaded what it meant, but stuck in her cockpit, she could only stew in fear.

As soon as she entered the large hanger, a bracket swung up and clamped the belly of her ship. The cockpit shuddered, and all sensation of movement stopped with a sudden twist of her guts. A heartbeat later, the ship rotated before it was yanked down one of the long, endless aisles between hundreds of ship bays. Each carried a fighter ship like her own.

The three minutes it took to bring her ship to its bay were the longest of her life. As the bracket swung her around and shoved the ship nose-first into the bay, she saw three people waiting for her.

She didn't recognize two of them, but they wore military police uniforms and stood at attention with unslung pulse rifles in their hands. They weren't smiling, but she didn't expect any compassion from her greeters.

But it was the third person that caused her stomach to twist violently. Her brother, Duncan, stood with his pistol at his side, a glare on his face, and his arms crossed over his chest. The black uniform of the military police shone in the light above him, revealing that he wore his armor to arrest his own sister. And was armed with the gun that she bought him for his latest promotion.

The feeling of dread rose as she levered herself out of her seat and slipped around. There was very little space behind the seat, enough to access the maintenance panels and not much else. Her feet scuffed against the diamond plate as she headed to the door.

It was already unlocked by the hanger bay computers, so she pushed it open and crawled out. She hesitated at the bottom of the ladder, unwilling to turn around and face her fate.

When she heard Duncan's boots on the ground, she forced herself to turn around.

"Third Lieutenant Midoze 73, you are to come with me." Her brother's voice didn't even waver as he made the announcement. They both shared the name, Midoze 73 for the Midoze genetic strain, 73rd generation since the asteroid ship first launched.

She took another deep breath and nodded, not trusting herself to speak.

Her brother turned and started down the hall. He didn't wait for her to follow.

The other two guards stepped aside, obviously expecting her to pass.

Eliza struggled to say something, anything, but then decided to remain silent and obey. Her boots squeaked on the plate as she walked quickly to catch up to her brother. She started to pull even with him, but a single glare forced her to slow down until she was pacing a meter behind him.

The four of them marched down the hall. Her hopes that Duncan would have picked a less populated hallway were crushed when he strode down the busiest corridor leaving the hanger. Crowds of pilots, maintenance crew, and officers stepped to the aside as they passed, adding to a rapidly growing humiliation that burned her cheeks.

To her despair, there were more than a few looks of glee as she passed. She knew she wasn't popular. She was one of the best pilots on the asteroid, but she was also one of the lowest ranking. Her "deviant actions" were legendary, though with a crew of humans suppressing their sexuality, getting caught giving a handjob was a legend.

That handjob cost her a promotion and sent her lover to the opposite end of the asteroid, but it was one of the greatest moments of her life.

"Third Lieutenant, this isn't a laughing matter."

Eliza's smile dropped from her face as she glared at her brother. "I didn't mean it."

Duncan stopped sharply and spun around to face her. "Mean what? Force an unauthorized medical diagnostics? Or violate every flight protocol we have?"

She stepped back but bumped into one of the police behind her. She looked and saw there was at least two dozen people staring at her.

"Or," he continued, "did you accidentally rip open your flight suit before accidentally," he spat out the word, "pleasuring yourself like some sort of animal!"

"No—"

"Because that sounds a lot like what you were doing!" His voice echoed loudly in the suddenly quiet hallway.

A prickle of annoyance rose up inside her. "At least I was doing something! Do you know how boring those flights are?"

Duncan stepped up, his shoulders almost even with her eyes. "You are an FCM pilot! Those missions are critical for our safety!"

"They are critical for keeping us from getting bored!"

"Obviously that isn't working!" He raised a fist, but didn't bring it down. His face twisted in a scowl before he stepped back. Clearing his throat, he turned. "The colonel demanded your presence."

He turned and strode forward. After a few minutes of walking, he stopped at an elevator bank and pressed his wrist against the control. The ETA of the nearest car turned red as his priority override turned it into an express elevator. A moment later, the door opened and she was pushed inside.

Eliza's armor creaked as she turned around, surrounded by the three police. Clearing her throat, she looked at her brother's back. "Duncan—"

"That's Captain Midoze, Lieutenant. Captain Midoze 73 if you want to be proper."

"Fine, Captain Midoze, let—"

"I didn't give you permission to speak."

She ground her jaw together. "Permission—"

"Denied."

"Damn—"

"Denied!"

She flinched at Duncan's bellow. Ducking her head, she stared at her boots for the remainder of the elevator trip.

Depressing seconds later, the door opened at the officer levels. They were the leaders, lawmakers, and judges of the asteroid ship. Ultimately, everyone reported to Ship General Poldin, but her chain of command started at Colonel Ritan, and she doubted she would ever see a higher rank.

The officer floors were silent and carpeted. Instead of the crowds in the main corridor, only a few uniformed individuals walked along the hallways. Eliza didn't see anyone ranked under a major.

Eliza struggled with her fears as she was marched down to the colonel's office. The muted thump of marching boots echoed her own steps. The sound felt like a death march to her own execution.

She had never been to the colonel's office, but there was no question about his power on the asteroid. The outer office was manned by a single secretary with a desk almost as large as Eliza's ship.

The dour-faced woman looked up as Duncan approached. She struck a button with one hand and said, "The colonel is expecting her."

Her. The woman spoke as if Eliza was a mere beast or an unintelligent animal. Eliza felt herself bristling at the tone, but there were far more terrifying things beyond the opening doors.

Colonel Ritan's office was a massive room larger than the ship bay. The entire back of the office showed a view of the stars beyond the horizon. She knew it wasn't glass; they wouldn't risk decompression to something as trivial as glass. If it wasn't for her record displayed twenty meters high behind him, she would have assumed it was transparent.

The picture to Ritan's right was an older one. She recognized the small, pert nose and dark eyes, but her hair was longer during her last promotion. There was so much joy and hope in her expression, a young girl who was just promoted to ship pilot. Her body was still slender, almost thin. Her breasts stood high underneath her black uniform, though only she knew how hard the nipples were below the thick fabric.

Duncan continued forward, and the police behind her shoved her forward.

Eliza whimpered softly in the back of her throat as she covered the thirty meters across the mirror-smooth floor to stand in front of the colonel's desk.

Colonel Ritan sat there, his eyes fixed on her and a scowl etched across his face. He looked the same as the last time she saw him—nine hours had done nothing for his mood.

Duncan and the military police snapped to attention. Eliza followed suit a heartbeat later, saluting properly and thankful that her hand was no longer dripping with her juices.

"Third Lieutenant Midoze 73." The colonel's voice scraped against her senses, a deep bass rumble that shook her to the core.

She blinked to avoid crying and straightened her back.

"For seven years, the FCM has invested a large amount of time, personnel, and training on you." He steepled his fingers and leaned forward. "And somehow, you have managed to insult us every step of the way."

Eliza shuddered and swallowed, her throat was dry.

"You have been demoted six times and have yet to gain a single net rank in that time. If it wasn't for your brother's recommendation," the colonel's eyes flickered to Duncan and back, "you would have been discharged years ago."

"I'm a good pilot, sir." She gulped with the realization she spoke out of turn.

"Yes," came the growl. "You rank in the top thousand of every pilot we've had in a hundred years. Your test scores are exemplary, and your tactics are above par."

She prayed it was enough.

"However, you are inflicted with a sickness."

The tightness in her chest and throat increased. She found it hard to breathe, but there was nothing she could do but hold her salute and wait.

"Unlike your brother, or anyone else on this ship, you are incapable of moving beyond your baser drives. Your libido has risked the safety of this ship, this crew, and everyone that depends on you."

Eliza wanted to say something. It wasn't wrong to enjoy pleasure. It was a part of being human to enjoy sex. It didn't matter if it was fingers or cock, she knew her body was built for it, just like everyone else.

She released her held breath. If she wanted to remain a pilot, her career depended on her keeping her mouth shut.

"With this realization, I would hope that you would have the honor to do the right thing and take a long walk out of one of the airlocks. In fact," he growled, "I'll even authorize you access to the airlocks for said walk—"

The computer at her wrist chirped in acknowledgment.

"—but time and time again, you have failed to understand what damage you are doing to the morale of the space fleet and the crew." He took a deep breath, and the silence was deafening. He stood up and brought his wrists behind his back.

"Third Lieutenant Midoze 73, you are hereby discharged of your duties as a space pilot and sentenced to two years of hard labor in the prison levels."

Eliza let out a sob and staggered. Her salute faltered.

"Stand straight!"

Tears running down her cheeks, she forced herself back up. She tried to lift her hand to her temple, but couldn't. Her sobs filled the room but didn't echo against the distant walls.

"In deference to your service and skills, you will be given a single opportunity to regain your former rank. If there is even one report of fornication, copulation, or deviant behavior on your record in two years, you will spend the rest of your life in prison."

He stared at her for a long moment before he continued. "In the rare chance that you somehow manage to keep your legs together and your mind pure, the same restrictions will apply to your resumed duties. As far as I'm concerned, if I see a single violation point cross my desk, you will never fly again."

Eliza drew in a gasping breath. She wanted to scream, cry, and throw herself at his feet for mercy. Everything inside her begged to turn to Duncan, but she knew her brother couldn't save her anymore.

"Do you understand, Prisoner Midoze 73?"

Barely able to see through the tears, she thought she nodded.

"You are dismissed."

Five Minutes

The bell rang out to indicate the end of Eliza's shift. The piercing noise cut through the sound of pneumatic hammers and saws. Even if she wasn't waiting for it, she would have felt it in the back of her teeth or through the buzz of her wrist computer.

The prisoners of her shift set down their equipment and stepped away from the ragged stone wall stretching the entire length of the asteroid. The following shift was already marching into place, their heads bowed down and their shoes barely shuffling along the rock.

Eliza used the back of her other wrist to wipe the sweat and rock dust from her brow. It left a smear of iron oxide along the skin. She shook her hand to clear it and gave an impersonal nod to her replacement, a thin-set man whom she barely knew.

"Shift four, return to barracks. Shift five, begin mining operations." The prison AI had a deep, commanding voice. It also spoke slow and monotone, giving no hint of personality besides the need to obey.

Eliza forced her face to remain slack as she marched in line with the other prisoners. Nine months ago, she suffered with constant randomization. Now, everything was scheduled to the second, and there was no variation to break the monotony. She worked every day, with a break every three weeks. Her times were enforced by prison AI and even her wrist computer, which had been wiped of everything but the prison programming.

It was five kilometers back to her barracks. She spent the entire time staring at the back of her neighbor, an older man given life for killing his son, and struggling to keep her mind blank. It was the only way she could survive the tedium.

In the corner of her eye, she could see the sensors activating as she passed. They were watching her, waiting for her to make a mistake. It didn't matter if she was in the bathroom, sleeping in bed, or walking down the corridor, the nearest sensors were always lit up and watching. If she made the mistake of scratching herself too long, it would beep in warning.

It took the prison line, a hundred men and women strong, an hour to reach the barracks. The cadence of their march never slowed or stopped, just the steady thump of a hundred feet hitting the ground at the same time.

She lifted her gaze as they passed through the threshold. Right at the entrance was the FCM's motto: "For the Greater Good."

The dense list of regulations and rules covered both sides of the hallway as they entered the barracks. She knew them by memory, but her eyes always drifted toward rule seven: no fornication.

Nine months without an orgasm.

She strained to keep her hands on her side and her eyes down.

"Shower rotation starts with seven."

Eliza's heart beat faster. She got to enjoy the first round of showers after a shift, one of the few pleasures of her new life. She stepped to the side and headed for the showers.

The smell of fresh steam brought an unwitting smile to her lips. She couldn't wait for the heated touch against her skin.

"You have five minutes remaining."

Eliza hurried up down the hallway and into the shower area. As she moved, she tugged her uniform off her shoulders and pulled it down over her waist. The moist, warm air rolled over her skin, and her body hummed with the thrill of being naked.

The other nineteen prisoners of Group Seven were doing the same thing. By the time they reached the locker area, they were all stripped and naked. She didn't look at any of them; they were all sweaty and dirty. It didn't matter if they were male or female; they were just bodies.

She jammed her uniform into the laundry chute and dove for the first open shower bay. Hot steam poured down on her as soon as she passed the threshold. It rolled down her face and along the curves of her body before being sucked into the vents at her feet.

Leaning over, she grabbed the next wash towel and pulled it free. The square tore off, already slick with soap. She wasn't allowed to touch herself, not with the sensors watching her. Instead, she closed her eyes and began to scrub herself down.

She started with her hair, buzz cut by regulations, and worked her way down. Thick rivers of rust and dirt poured down her body, following the lines of her breasts, hips, and thighs. The caress against her neglected skin brought a quickening to her heart, a torture when she was forbidden to do anything beyond suffer with the tiny caresses of forbidden pleasure.

She brought the washcloth over her breasts, swiping at them even as her nipples ached to be rubbed. The rasp of the soapy fabric sent little thrills across her skin, and she clenched her muscles to remain standing. Taking a risk, she swiped it underneath the swells and then up to drag the fabric against her nipples.

The sensor bar next to her beeped in warning.

Eliza snatched her hand away and forced herself to work down. The heated end of the washcloth stroked along her belly, hard from months of labor, and then over her hips and ass. She scrubbed her rear carefully before wringing out the cloth.

She bit her lip and closed her eyes, steeling herself for the next part. With a lean to the side, she opened up her legs and drew the cloth in a single swipe from clitoris to ass, dragging the fabric through the thin patch of hair guarding her entrance.

Regulations required her to clean her privates, but the torturous pleasure of feeling friction against her clit was almost too much. She knew her heart was beating faster, and the sensors were wary of any violation of pleasure.

When she didn't hear a beep, she let out a sigh and continued down her thighs. She bent over to scrub, but also to hide the tears sparkling in her eyes.

It had been nine months of hell.

More than once, she considered using her wrist computer to open the airlock and kill herself, but she couldn't. Instead, she suffered through the terror of her nightly showers and unceasing life.

"You have one minute remaining."

A Reprieve

It felt strange not to be working, even for a single day. Eliza tugged her prison uniform along her body, straightening the fastener so it made a straight line from her throat to her crotch. The bright yellow fabric, brittle from daily washes and poor material, crinkled over her breasts even as it stretched over the peaks of her nipples. She tugged at it again, but the fabric scraped over her sensitive skin and she winced from the discomfort.

Her wrist computer finished rebooting with a chime. Curious, she glanced over and watched as the full-color display came to life. A smile stretched across her face just at seeing options once again. For the last ten months, her AI-controlled computer had a single button to call for help and a clock. Now, it had almost all of the controls, excluding shopping of course. The clock was still there, but so was a countdown for the remaining seconds before she was once again a prisoner.

"Prisoner Midoze 73, you have been granted nineteen hours of reprieve." She could almost imagine the prison AI sounded sad at the announcement. "You are required to return to this point before the period has expired, otherwise you will be arrested and your prison sentence extended one hour for every missed second. Do you understand?"

"Y-Yes." Eliza winced at her voice; it was rough from not talking.

"Enjoy."

She looked up sharply at the nearest sensor bar, surprised at the last word. The AI said nothing else, but the light remained watching her.

Suddenly self-conscious, she ran her hands through her freshly washed hair and shifted her body in the loose uniform. Her body felt tight, though she wasn't sure if it was from muscles hardened by heavy labor or the nervousness of walking among the others. She only wished her uniform was any color other than the bright yellow of the prison levels. She longed for the somber blacks and grays, even the dark blue and greens.

She took a deep breath. And then another. Steeling herself, she started down the hall toward the elevator that would bring her up from the bowels of the asteroid to the populated areas. She expected it to refuse to open for her, but it opened smoothly as she approached.

At the prison level, there were no options. The doors closed and the elevator rose out of the depths of the asteroid and back into civilization. She stared at the numbers, each floor representing years of work by labors as they cannibalized their home for minerals and raw matter. She felt like some parasite as she watched the numbers rise.

When the door opened to a secondary corridor, a wave of noise rolled into the elevator car. People talked. Even in the muted respectful tones of civilization, it was a far cry from the enforced silence in the barracks. Eliza winced and stepped back. She felt like a little girl again, terrified to venture out among the others.

Duncan stepped into view. He wore his off-duty uniform, which was still black, and a smile. Holding out his hand, he said, "Eliza."

A sob rose in her throat. Eliza stumbled forward and threw herself at him, hugging him tightly.

He wrapped his arms around her, rocking her back and forth as he held her tight. "It's okay, it's going to be okay."

"I'm sorry." She blinked at the tears.

"Wow, you sound...." He stopped, but she felt a sharp stab of guilt. She knew Duncan; he would try to avoid talking about her sentence.

Giggling softly, she wiped her face and pulled back. "They don't let us talk that much," she rasped, "makes it hard when we come back. I wasn't sure I'd even get any words out."

Duncan smiled. He reached up and ran his hands through her short hair, the short strands caught his palm in a cascade. His hand was firm but shaking.

She shivered. It felt good to have anyone touch her, even if it was her own brother.

"I liked it a bit longer."

Eliza nodded, unsure of her voice.

"Soon, right?"

Another nod. "I-I hope so," she said in a quiet voice.

"It isn't so bad, is it?"

She opened her mouth to agree, but couldn't. Every day, she feared and craved the showers and her own bed. She wanted to touch herself, to feel some human contact, but couldn't. Prisoners weren't allowed to talk to each other, much less touch. Instead of answering, she closed her mouth and glanced at the nearest sensor strip. It was lit up, an ever-present eye for her to make a single mistake.

Duncan cleared his throat. "Breakfast?"

Grateful for the segue, she nodded.

He offered his arm and she took it. For a moment, the contrast was painful, the somber black of a captain in the military police and the bright yellow of a disgraced pilot. She stared down at their arms and felt the tears rise up.

"No, no," Duncan whispered. "Don't think about that. Come on, my treat."

She looked at him and smirked. She let him guide her down the corridor to a less restricted elevator bank.

As they walked, people turned to stare. She could feel their eyes on her skin, but there was nothing she could do. She was still a prisoner on the ship, though she had a day to pretend otherwise.

The sensor bar also lit up, following her movements.

To her surprise, Duncan took her to the captain's mess. She had only been there once, when he was promoted. At the door, she came to a stumbling halt and stared at the cloth draped tables and crystal glasses. Most of the tables were empty, but she saw uniformed officers eating with silver flatware at tables scattered around the room. A blush on her cheeks, she tugged at his arm. "Duncan!"

"What?"

"You can't take me in here! This is for officers!"

"Yes, I can. I'm an officer."

"I-I'm a—"

"My sister. And it's quiet; no one will say anything."

"But," her voice dropped to a whisper, "what about this?" She gestured to her bright yellow uniform. Compared to the rest of the room and the somber shades of the military, she was almost blinding in brilliance.

Duncan smiled and pulled her in. "Captain's prerogative. Come, you need a good meal and I'm suspecting you can't handle the normal richness you used to eat. Or the noise."

Not entirely unwilling, Eliza let herself be guided to one of the tables and sat down. The fabric underneath her callused palms felt like silk, and she stroked her palms along it, getting pleasure from the texture itself. When she imagined it against her bare skin, she felt the blush rise on her cheeks.

Duncan pushed her chair in before sitting himself. "I figured you'd needed a little pampering. I hope you don't mind."

"Thank you."

A waiter came up in his gray uniform. His eyes grazed over Eliza before he focused on Duncan. "How may I serve you, Captain?"

"Two glasses of white wine, please."

A muscle in the waiter's cheek jumped. "Excuse me, captain, but regulations state that—"

"I'm aware of the regulations." The smile faded from Duncan's face. "I'm also aware that I'm allowed to disregard them in situations that I deem important. And today, I do. Two glasses. That's an order."

"Yes, sir," the waiter said in a tone of disapproval.

Eliza waited until the waiter had left before she giggled. "You know prisoners aren't supposed to have alcohol."

Duncan smirked and raised an eyebrow. "I also remember that, as captain, I'm allowed to dispense with that rule. But, within moderation. So, this is your one and only glass of wine."

"Thank you... Duncan."

He nodded. "You're a good girl, Eliza, don't forget that. I know life is hard, but I know you can do this."

"No, I can't."

"Yes. Just find something to be passionate about."

"Isn't that my problem? Being passionate?"

"Okay," he said as he rolled his eyes, "not that type of passion. I mean something to believe in, something that you throw your entire heart into. I know you can and," he smiled, "when you do, life won't be so bad."

She couldn't find the words to say. Instead, she stared down at her rough fingers, tracing the scars from shards of rocks and calluses from the jackhammers. The muscles in her arms were hard and corded, not quite bulging, but months of labor had given her a harshness that she found both erotic and disturbing at the same time.

A minute later, the waiter returned with the wine and poured the glasses. Duncan ordered for both of them, and the waiter left in a hurry.

Eliza toyed with the glass for a moment, watching the waiter disappear into the kitchen. She noticed others, mostly administrative assistants currently serving the other officers, watching her. Shamed, she turned away and focused on her untouched wine. "Duncan?"

"Yes?"

"Why are you doing this?"

"Doing what?"

She lifted her gaze. He was staring at her, his brown eyes almost piercing. "Being nice. The other Midozes don't talk to me or even want to be near me. The 73s do the same. I don't even have friends among the 72s and 74s. Why you? Why haven't you... given up me like everyone else?"

He set down his glass. "You remember when we got locked in the pantry for a day? When Galfin 70 didn't realize we were eating all the chocolate?"

"Of course. But, that was twenty years ago."

"I made a promise."

"You were four."

"We were four," he said with a smile, "and I keep my promises. There is something about you, Eliza, something that the other Midozes and 73s don't have. Something all the 70s don't have. It's...

it's..." He waved his hand. "I can't explain it, but it kills me to see you suffer."

"I try, I really do."

He reached out and cradled his hands. He had the soft grip of a man who never touched anything rougher than his keyboard. It felt like silk against her scars. She expected him to draw back, but he caressed the side of her palm with his thumb. "You are my sister. I know it means less since we were simply in the same batch of tubes, but it's true."

She took a deep breath. "Were you the reason I only have two years of this?"

His hand tightened for a moment and then relaxed.

Eliza glanced up at him. There was guilt in his eyes.

With a sinking feeling, she figured it out. "You were the one who suggested it, weren't you?"

Duncan pulled his hand back and looked away. "They were..." He took a deep breath before continuing. "Going to make a terrible mistake."

She closed her eyes. "Execution? All because I touched myself?"

"I'm sorry."

"Thank you, I guess," she managed to croak as despair crushed her. She hated the world around her. The military, who controlled the entire ship, was strict and controlling. The idea that stealing a bit of pleasure would be an executable offense wasn't new to her, but the knowledge of how close she was to dying twisted her insides. "I'm flawed, aren't I?"

"Aren't we all?"

She shook her head, a bitter smile on her lips. "No, you aren't. You are the perfect soldier here. You obey without question and everyone knows you'll end up Admiral of the Ship."

"I'm sure I'll disobey an order." He coughed sheepishly.

Eliza glared at him.

"Okay, I don't disobey but... Eliza... you know you can do the same thing. You just have—"

"No," she whispered. "I can't. I've tried." She stared at the glass, watching as condensation dripped along the outer curve and splashed on her hand.

Duncan said nothing for a long moment.

Eliza sipped at her glass before she finally looked up again.

He wasn't looking at her anymore. Instead, his gaze focused over her shoulder.

Confused, Eliza turned around.

"Don't scream," Duncan said sharply.

She glanced at him. "What?"

"It's one, no, two of the raptors."

"A raptor?" She turned back around. "What's a raptor?"

At the entrance to the officer's mess, she saw a thick knot of military. The black uniforms were the only color visible, with silver and gold trim marking the ranks. Among a dozen aides, she spotted a colonel and a major general.

"Duncan? I don't see—" Her voice froze as a flash of brilliant color rose up above the heads of the crew. It was bright red with streaks of yellow, the contrast to the black uniforms almost blinding.

Eliza inhaled sharply as the head continued to rise. It was elongated and about twice the size of a human's. It continued down a supine neck hidden by the uniformed bodies. The alien—it wasn't human—had two, bright blue eyes on each side of its head, and she could see teeth peeking out from thin lips.

"We call them raptors," Duncan said, "but that's not what they call themselves. The computer is still struggling with the linguistics of their language so we don't have a better name. They showed up near the asteroid about a month ago. They have a huge fleet with some sort of jump drive, but we don't know how it works or even their intentions."

She looked back at him. "Who found them?"

"First Lieutenant Lassin 74."

"And he probably shot them, right?"

"Yeah," Duncan sighed. "And then the raptors shot back. Lassin didn't make it, and we had a couple battles out there before everyone calmed down."

She sighed. "I wish I was there."

He chuckled. "If you were flying, we would have won. You're one of the best fighter pilots out there and you wouldn't have been bored with that."

"Of course I'm the best, I'm a Midoze." With a grin, she turned back to the crowd. The raptor had stepped out from the crowd. It was a lizard with a long sweeping tail. It looked about six meters long but only stood three high. It stretched a meter above the rest of the humans. Its back legs were massive, and it looked strong enough to cut through metal with the long claws that tipped its feet and hands.

The raptor tilted its head and looked around the room. She cringed as the bright blue caught hers. For a moment, it felt like it was staring at her like a hunk of meat, but then it continued to peer around the room.

"That's Fleet Master Kraken. He's in charge of the entire fleet."

"He's...." Eliza couldn't find the words. The raptor was something she had never seen before or even imagined existing. He was bright, huge, and utterly new. She wanted to reach out and touch him, just to run her hand along his pebbled skin or look closely into the brilliant eyes.

"You know, if things go well, we'll still be allies with the raptor fleet when you finish your prison sentence."

Eliza turned, her mouth dropping in shock.

Duncan smiled. "You know, if you need something new to be passionate about."

An Unexpected Pardon 5

Eliza planted her boot on the side of the wall and gripped her rock hammer with both hands. The thirty kilogram sledge strained her back and shoulders, but she swung it up and over her head to bring it down on the spike sticking out of the wall.

The ringing impact pierced the din of jackhammers and pneumatic drills. Rock shattered as the spike pried a large slab of iron ferrite from the tunnel wall. Rust and dust cascaded down the rough surface as she swung the sledge around again to strike the spike.

The steady ring of her hammer was deafening. Each burst echoed off transparent shields erected around her to prevent shrapnel from injuring the other prisoners. She tried not to think about being sacrificed as she drove the spike deeper.

It had been three months since her day of reprieve. Somehow, she managed to sink into a world of despair where she didn't crave the touch of her own fingers or another being. She knew, deep in her core, she was killing herself, but every time her willpower began to crack, she thought about the raptor.

He was something new. Probably the only new thing she would ever experience in her life. The unceasing pseudo-randomness of being a pilot or the strict schedule of a prisoner were her cage. The raptor, though utterly alien, promised memories that would keep for the rest of her life. It didn't matter if she never flew again; she just wanted to meet the alien.

The haft of the sledge scraped along her palm and tugged at her work gloves. She swung it around and drove it hard into the spike. The heat of the hardened metal disappeared into the crack, and the hammer bounced off the rock.

She stepped back to follow the swing and to avoid hurting herself. As the head came down, she dropped it to the ground and felt the shudder impact through her feet. Turning back around, she leaned the sledge against the wall. Her hands shook from her exhaustion, and her sweat soaked her uniform. The bright yellow fabric had darkened in the last few hours from sweat and blood. She was sure it was glued to her body from her efforts.

Rubbing her hands, she stepped back until she could press her back against the shield. Then, she stepped sideways and around the other side, planting herself in the space between the shield and the opposite wall of the tunnel.

Her thighs and arms burned and itched. She glance down at her torn uniform where shards of rock had cut through it and scored the skin below. The scratches would only add to the network of scars she had acquired in the last year of mining.

Taking a deep breath, she rotated her wrist. For today's duties, she had a few more options, but they were strictly limited to her tasks. She swiped through the warnings and brought up the control system for the low-speed explosives in the seven spikes she rammed behind the slab. She winced before she tapped the button.

The wall exploded out, the concussion force slamming into the shields and the muffled boom punching her in the gut.

As the dust settled, she saw the slab of iron slowly peeling away from the wall. Smoke rose out from the blackened crack and it swirled around the edges as the slab swung out and then rocketed to the ground.

A five hundred kilogram hunk of iron punched the ground. The impact shook the stone floor, and she felt it rolling away from her.

Eliza wanted to feel some joy at her accomplishment, but she only had four hours left to break it into small enough pieces for the next shift to move it. She used the back of her arm to smear the sweat across her brow and away from her eyes.

"Prisoner Midoze 73!"

At her name, she jumped. She looked up reflexively, to the sensor bar which still shone down on her. But, the speakers weren't activated. Confused, she lowered her gaze and scanned down one direction of the tunnel before looking behind her.

They were waiting for her: three military police in black uniforms just acquiring a thin layer of dust. They were all armed, but their weapons were holstered. Two of them were staff sergeants, but the lead one, a broad-shouldered man with black hair, had a captain's insignia on his uniform.

The captain gestured for her to approach.

She hesitated and looked at the sensor bar.

"Midoze 73!" bellowed the captain over the din.

Flinching, Eliza pushed herself away from the shield and her slab of iron. Her footsteps were unheard in the din, but she felt every step as she left her assigned spot.

Exactly six hundred centimeters from the shield, her wrist computer flashed red. "Notice!" boomed the AI computer, "Prisoner Midoze 73, return to your position. You have ten seconds to comply. Failure to obey will result in immediate punishment."

The corridor grew quieter as the speaker repeated itself even louder.

The officer held up his hand. "Override, authorization order 238853."

"Processing... override accepted."

Her computer stopped beeping, but the sensor bars that watched her remained lit and focused on her. She continued to walk toward the captain and felt the lights moving to trace her movements.

The captain looked her from head to toe. "Come on."

"What's wrong?"

He glared. "Come."

"Can I get—?" His look stopped her dead in her tracks. "Yes, sir."

The captain turned and strode down the tunnel. The prisoners parted around him but didn't look away from their duties.

Eliza followed. She knew they were focused on her, mostly with curiosity, but they had mastered the art of paying attention while appearing to work. She kept her back straight despise her exhaustion and hurried along.

The nearest elevator was a quarter kilometer away. She could make it easily, but she noticed the sergeants behind her struggled to keep up with her rapid pace. She felt almost a vicious joy and wanted to walk faster, but the captain in front of her prevented it.

Instead, she worried about why three military police were picking her up. She hadn't touched herself in months. In her shower, she used exactly one stroke for each breast, one for her pussy, and one for her ass. It was the only way she could get through the days.

Her nervousness only increased when they reached the elevator and entered it without another word. The doors closed and the cool air washed over her, prickling the sweat along her skin and causing the multitude of scratches and cuts to throb. She shivered as she watched the numbers rapidly decrease. The outermost layer of the asteroid was 0 and the prison was currently on 119.

Squirming in nervousness and discomfort, Eliza could feel the others focusing on her, and their attention added to the discomfort that the ever-present sensor bar gave her. She imagined they saw her as flawed genetic material, an insult to everything the FCM represented. A shiver coursed along her muscles and she closed her eyes until the elevator slowed.

It opened on the nineteenth floor, one of the many levels reserved for higher-ranking officers.

The doors opened to silence. The familiar smell of sweat, dust, and oil was gone. Instead, she could only smell perfume and air fresheners. She hesitated to leave the elevator car, but the two sergeants behind her pushed her forward.

Dirt and grime cascaded off her uniform as she was marched down the hallway. A long time ago, she knew the floor, but after a year, there was only a sense of vague familiarity and a growing sense of fear. She wanted Duncan to be there, if anything to give an easy smile.

They stopped at a door. She had a few seconds to see the symbol on the door before they opened it. It was Master Colonel Ritan. Any hope was dashed almost instantly, and she let out a shuddering breath.

The captain marched through the entry office.

The same secretary sat behind the desk. She pressed the same button to open the door, and Eliza couldn't tell if her face even moved in the year and a half since Eliza had been sentenced to prison.

Master Colonel Ritan's expression had also not changed since she last saw him. The only difference was the picture projected on the massive display behind him. It was her in a yellow uniform, the day she was sentenced to prison. Her red-rimmed eyes glistened with tears as the video played a five second clip of her sobbing.

She wondered what she looked like now. Would her eyes be dead? Her spirit crushed by endless work and terror?

Ritan gestured to the police. "Leave us."

"Yes, sir," came the reply from all three. A few seconds later, she was alone with the man who sentenced her to years in prison. She struggled with her urge to turn and make for the door. She knew it would be locked, but she didn't want to be anywhere near Ritan.

Ritan's scowl deepened into thick furrows of anger. He gestured in front of his massive desk. "Approach."

Eliza walked closer. The large office was terrifying, but the time it took for her to reach his desk only magnified her fear. Every step was agony, the pulse on her neck throbbed with every ragged breath.

When she stopped in the assigned spot, a hunk of iron fell from the folds of her uniform and hit the ground. It rang out before settling at her feet. She glanced down, trying to see if she could pick it up.

"Leave it," said Ritan.

She straightened.

Ritan looked her over. "Prisoners salute first."

Eliza felt the despair clawing at her heart and raised her hand in a salute. The side of her hand trembled as she held it in place. She could feel the tears burning her eyes, but fought to prevent them from rolling down her cheeks.

Ritan swiped his desk and lights faded underneath his palm. He steepened his fingers as he regarded her. "I don't like you."

She could feel the muscles in her neck and back burning.

"I would have had you executed years ago. You are disgrace to this asteroid, this military, and common decency everywhere. The FCM *Quantor* set out to escape people like you, obsessed with filth and unable to rise above animistic urges."

There was nothing she could say to respond.

"If it was your genetic stock, I would have had the entire Midoze line destroyed, but the rest of your... kind has talents we need. You excel at marksmanship and piloting, along with a loyalty that is sadly misplaced in your brother. These all make your ancestry commendable, but also identifies you a singularly flawed and diseased individual." His hard, brutal words punched her with every syllable. He never raised his voice, his anger bristled with every word from his mouth.

He sighed and shook his head. "I had hoped you would have saved me the trouble, but, I'm sad to say, I am now glad that you didn't have the decency to walk out that airlock."

Eliza focused sharply on the man.

Ritan straightened his back and tapped his desk. On the left side of his display, opposite of her portrait, two symbols appeared. She knew the top one, it was a captain's insignia, but she didn't know the subdivision. Below was the prison mark, the same as the one on her uniform.

He shook his head again. "I can't believe it's come to this. Eliza, 73rd Generation of the Midoze genetic line, by orders of the Admiral of the Ship, you have been given two choices."

"T-Two?" she gasped.

His glare silenced her. "Yes, two. And you will make the choice before you leave this room." A muscle in his jaw tightened. "The first is the easiest, return to prison. Your sentence will be extended for the rest of your life, without any chance of parole."

She exhaled with a sob. She had tried so hard not to earn a single violation. Months of torture and struggle and then Ritan just ripped away all her hope in a single instance.

"Stop crying, it's pathetic. The second, is... is..." He growled for a moment. "It's a promotion to major captain, effective immediately for a special assignment."

Eliza was kneeling on the ground before she realized she had fallen. Her body trembled from the impact but she couldn't do anything but sob loudly. The tears were red with rust as they splattered on the ground and soaked her uniform.

"Get up."

She couldn't. "W-Why?"

Ritan cleared his throat. After a moment, he did it again. Then, his chair scraped on the floor before his footsteps came around the desk.

"Because, while you are expendable, protocol requires a liaison to be a captain."

She looked up at him, barely able to see through the tears that blurred her vision. "Liaison?"

"Yes, with Fleet Master Kraken and the raptor fleet." There was almost a smile. "To be honest, it's a suicide mission."

"I-I don't understand."

"You know about the raptor fleet, the sentient dinosaurs that approached five months ago?"

She nodded.

"Of course you do, your psychological profile indicated that your brief view of Kraken and your brother's words were a turning point in resisting your flawed libido."

He leaned on his desk. "We've had two liaison officers with the fleet since then. Both of them were murdered," a smile crossed his face, "and, in Madden 75's case, eaten. We're not entirely sure how it happened, other than the fleet is manned by carnivorous creatures that have no discipline or self-control."

Eliza whimpered.

"However, in both cases, the fleet has apologized to the FCM by gifting us an impressive portfolio of technology. So," his smile broadened, "my hopes is that you will be torn to pieces and the raptors will give us access to their jump drives."

"A-A sacrifice? You're sacrificing me?"

"Yes," he said in a dead-panned tone. "I can think it is the only use for your flawed genetics. Your death will benefit everyone for generations to come."

Staring at him in shock, she couldn't find the words. She wanted to tear out his throat, but she knew the automated defense systems would stop her before she covered the meter between them. She gulped and tried to imagine being torn apart by the raptor she saw. To her surprise, her heart began to thump faster.

"Take the mission, girl."

"To die?"

"Yes," his lips tightened, "but there is more. The Admiral of the Ship has authorized your genetic line to be maintained in the case of your death in service to the ship and the greater good of the FCM."

"The greater good," she muttered.

"You will also have a corresponding increase in social benefits, both for your duties as Major Captain but also for the additional obligations of a liaison."

"Additional obligations?"

"Yes, your job is to interface between the fleets and the FCM. You will provide Kraken with any services he requires. If his requests are reasonable, you are to provide the proper paperwork and go through the procedures on his behalf. Likewise, if we require information, it is your responsibility for providing it, by their own protocols or by any means necessary."

Eliza frowned for a moment. "That last one sounds a lot like spying."

"It is spying," he said, "and probably why you will be killed in some bloody, hopefully painful, manner when your clumsy attempts at information gathering put you in the wrong place with no chance of rescue. But, in the odd chance you succeed, the FCM needs to know their long-term intentions, capabilities, and weaknesses. And you," he said with a cruel grin, "are the perfect person. Either you are murdered or you provide us with information. Either way, the FCM wins."

Ritan looked her over as she struggled with the choice. There was no way she would return to prison for life. Even the idea of being torn apart was far better than a lifetime of agony.

"One more thing. The sensor monitor will continue. I will not have you ruining the tenuous relationship with the raptors because you are unable to control your libido. If you have a single violation, I will order your execution personally."

She struggled with a response, her mouth opening and closing.

Ritan stared at her for a moment and then he started back around his desk. "Stand up, Major Captain, at least pretend you have some sort of pride."

Around her wrist, her computer beeped once as the AI computer began to program it for her new role. Apparently, her explicit consent wasn't needed, though she already knew she couldn't go back to the prison. Death was nothing compared to being broken.

6 Armed

Eliza tugged on her new uniform. She had never had tailored clothes before, and she had to admit the woman in the mirror looked alluring. Hard labor had given her a sharp, trim figure. It filled her suit almost perfectly, the black fabric following the curves of her small but perky breasts and the narrowness of her waist. The uniform was a formal one, with a straight skirt that barely covered her knees and a cut that encouraged her to keep her legs together. It was pitch black, with a dark blue collar and cuffs.

Her gaze lifted to her face. She could see the scars from her prison sentence, the faint white lines of scratches that came from flying rocks and shrapnel. Her eyes, the characteristic Midoze Brown, looked faded to her, dull and broken.

The very idea of dressing up to be killed terrified her, but it never reached her eyes. She wondered if she could ever smile again.

Her computer wrist chirpped to warn her about her appointment. She glanced down at the screen before straightening her outfit one last time and heading out of her quarters.

The new rank came with a richly appointed room, one that felt excessively large after spending months in a sleep coffin. It had only been three days since she accepted her rank, and she still wasn't used to having a bed.

Outside her quarters, she strode down the hallway to the nearest elevator. Her shoes, with five centimeter heels, tapped loudly along the smooth surface of the hallway as she joined others waiting for the lifts.

When the doors opened, Duncan stepped out with a smile. "Captain."

She smiled and twisted her hip. "Captain."

"Oh," he said. "Major Captain."

Eliza rolled her eyes. "Captain." He was still a few ranks above her.

He stepped in front of her to block her entering the car. "Give me a moment? In private? I was hoping to meet you in your room before you left."

She peeked up at him through her lashes. "I have to present myself to the Fleet Master in twenty-two minutes."

Duncan pressed his lips into a thin line, then gestured down the hall. "Just a second, then."

"Sure."

He took her away from the elevator. Turning his back to the hall, he dug into his jacket and pulled out a bundle. It wasn't a bag, but a rough, black material that reminded her of his holster. She glanced down at his sidearm, still at his side, and then looked up with a question.

"Yes, it's a Markon VI. Just like the one you got me."

"I'm supposed to be a liasion, Duncan. I don't think—"

"Two people died in that position. I don't care what they told you, I don't want to lose my sister to those... creatures." As he spoke, he unfolded the holster and slipped the energy pistol from its cradle. "Put that on."

Eliza stared at the black material for a moment, then obeyed. She slipped it around her waist and buckled it. When Duncan handed her gun, she inspected the charge. Seeing it full, she slipped it into the holster and flipped the thumbreak strap into place.

Taking a deep breath, she stood straight. "How do I look?"

Duncan looked her over. "Like I didn't do enough to save you."

"Save me?"

"I fought against this appointment, Eliza. I swear I did. But, Ritan had gone straight to the Admiralty after we got... after the last one was killed. By the time I came in, the orders were already set, and I couldn't do anything."

The reminder that the position was suicide struck her again. She rested her hand on her gun, wondering if it would somehow save her. She forced her fingers off it and hugged Duncan, who stiffened at the public display of affection. "Thank you, Duncan."

He coughed as he extricated himself. "Come on, the fleet master is waiting for you."

She nodded and patted her gun. "I'm ready."

"Just... don't use it on Ritan, okay?"

Giggling, she followed him back to the elevator. Now that he mentioned it, Eliza thought it was a good idea.

The Raptors

She and Duncan reached the meeting room within fifteen seconds of their appointment. They walked in step as they reached the door and then continued through it when it opened with their approach.

The meeting room was large, about six meters by five, but it felt small with the presence of three raptors and ten humans.

Fleet Master Kraken dwarfed the other two raptors. The three meter tall creature was a brilliant crimson among the black uniforms of the FCM personal. She knew him from her lessons, but the sight of an alien quickened her heart. His pebbled skin was two shades of red, darker on top with a paler patch from his throat to the bottom of his tail. Yellow stripes slashed across his back, going from the middle of his body down to his tail. She couldn't see stripes underneath the vest he wore, but intelligence said the strips went from neck to tail.

Her eyes flickered along the underbelly of the raptors. They didn't cover their bodies like the humans and she couldn't help but look at the ridge of the creature's pubic area. Or where she thought it would be. Military Intelligence gave no information about their mating habits, though she didn't dare ask how the raptors reproduced.

Realizing where her thoughts were going, Eliza forced her attention up to the faces of the aliens. Humans weren't interested in the baser urges like sex. That lesson had been pounded into her since the day she was born in a tube and brought up every time her flaws forced her into decisions she would later regret.

Eliza knew the identity of the other two raptors in the room, but like the bulk of the humans in the room, they were aides and functionaries. The male was Gornak and the female called herself Hissa.

They were important, but not as critical as the two highest ranking individuals: Kraken and Ritan.

Next to her, Duncan inhaled sharply. "We better introduce ourselves."

She nodded. Together, they made way across the room. With every step, she felt her heart pounding harder and faster. She only had one chance not to humiliate herself and she wasn't sure she could do it.

As they approach, Ritan saw her and put on a false smile. She could see how he strained to keep the ends of his mouth turned up. It didn't reach his eyes at all and she felt a shiver of fear at the man who held her life in his grip. "Ah, Fleet Master Kraken, I would like to introduce you to Captains Duncan and Eliza Midoze 73."

The massive creature turned his head to look at them with one brilliantly blue eye. Unlike humans, the lizard-like alien's eyes were situated on the side of its head.

Eliza shivered in the glare, wondering what he saw when he peered at her. She gulped and smiled back, a smile that was a lot more genuine that Ritan's.

"Rit-tan 69," Kraken's voice was a low rumble, and Eliza felt it in her belly. "Why you bring meat to me once again?"

Ritan's smile grew more strained. "These aren't meat. These are captains in the FCM. Some of my finest. And it's Ritan."

"They share name. Are they mated?" Kraken's eyes never turned away from Eliza's.

She found herself lost in the azure gaze. A quiver rolled through her body, but she didn't have a name for the emotion. It wasn't fear, that much she knew, but maybe anticipation. For her entire life, there was nothing to look forward to. Now, there was something new and exciting.

"No!" Ritan said sharply. "They are siblings."

"Ah, nest mate. I do not understand you generation number. I see their similarity. Dark hair, slender body. They are Midoze? A bloodline? I have not seen one with that name before."

"Yes," said Ritan, "from the 73rd generation. The Midoze line is," he glanced at Eliza, "distinctive in the FCM. They specialize in piloting and tactics."

"Is good." Kraken's lip pulled back to reveal a line of sharp, dusky teeth. Eliza's stomach tightened at the sharp points and she felt a quiver when Kraken licked his large incisors. "Both are my liaison?"

"Eliza here," Ritan gestured for her to step forward, "will be your liaison. She is highly qualified in this regard. Duncan is now in charge of your security while on the FCM *Quantor*."

Eliza stepped forward, praying that she wasn't sweating too hard. She opened her mouth to say something, but Kraken interrupted her with a laugh, a barking noise that the other raptors mimicked.

"More meat? Why do you keep assigning food to me?"

"I'm not meat." She spoke before she realized it. Her body was tense and shaking, but she stared into his blue eye.

From the corner of her eye, she saw Ritan's face turn red.

"Oh?" Kraken said. He leaned forward until his nostrils hovered millimeters from her nose. Her own pulse bridged the gap and their bodies touched. He was dry but somehow soft as leather. She could feel his incisor press against her skin. "You look like meat. You smell," he took a deep breath and it tickled her hair, "like meat. So, how can you not be meat?"

Her first touch against the raptor was electric, the sensations intensified by her fear. His skin rasped against her own and she knew that he could easily rip her head off with a moment's heartbeat. She straightened her back and stared at the blue eye centimeters away from my own. "Because, meat gives up."

Kraken pulled back, his teeth sparkling. "Ah, so the meat think." He laughed and tilted his head to look down. "At least this meat learn from previous mistake and bring claw to the fight."

Eliza followed his gaze to her pistol. She wasn't expecting him to point it out. Looking up, she glanced at Duncan who made a minute shake of his head. Turning, she saw Ritan snarling silently at her. She blanched and turned away.

Kraken laughed again. His voice, the low growl, filled the room as he raised it. "Rit-tan 69, this meat is not your favorite?"

Ritan did a double take. "E-Excuse me?"

"You pretend to smile at her. Your mouth say you are proud, your body say you dislike. When you forget I can see you, you snarl and turn red. Are you giving us poisoned meat?"

Ritan sputtered for a moment. "I-I can get someone else, if you want."

Kraken's smile grew. "No, I want to know this meat who speak back. She soft like other, but there is fight there. Maybe she not get killed with sneaking into place she do not belong? Yes? Is she a spy too? Trying to find fleet secret?"

Ritan's face grew redder but he said nothing.

Sensing the situation growing out of control, Eliza cleared her throat and shivered as the Fleet Master turned to her. "Um, my duties do not include spying, if that is what you ask. I'm here to act as a proxy of the FCM services to help ensure your stay is comfortable." It was the words they told her to say, except for the bit about spying. She wasn't suppose to mention that at all and she could feel Ritan glaring knives at her.

Kraken laughed. "The spy never claim to spy. But, we will see. Hopefully, I not find you torn apart in a tunnel, yes?"

"I have no intention of being torn apart, ever."

"Good, good. Now, Rit-tan 69, you be trusting your spy to do her job."

One of the human aides coughed uncomfortably.

The door to the room slid open as aides brought in platters of food. Eliza's stomach rumbled at the scents of roasted meat that filled the room.

"Eliza 73."

She shivered as Kraken addressed her. "Yes, sir?"

"You sit by me."

Ritan shook his head. "No, that isn't proper."

"She be liaison, yes?"

"Y-Yes."

"Then, she sit by me." Kraken's voice rumbled with a deeper growl. "Her duties can start immediately."

"Of course, Fleet Master."

Eliza followed Kraken around the table to where the raptors were placed. The raptors were too large for chairs, so the waiters had left a space clear for them. But, it was obvious that no human had sat near them. She started to look for a chair to drag over, then stopped.

She knew the protocols for sitting with higher ranked officers, but she also knew that she needed to make the raptors comfortable.

Kraken stopped in a spot and simply waited as the waiters served him.

She moved next to him, his left side according to protocol, and stood there.

Another of the raptors moved up to her other side and she felt very tiny between the two carnivorous aliens.

Kraken tilted his head to her. "You not need chair?"

She looked up at the massive creature. There were no lessons or instructions on what she was doing, but it felt right to her. "If you aren't sitting, I thought you would be more comfortable if I did the same."

The aide on her other side barked a laugh.

Kraken laughed himself. "Yes, the meat has compassion for those different. Please, stay standing. I like. No one else consider this before. Not in four of your month."

Eliza gulped and realized she was holding her breath. She let it out through her teeth.

Across the table, Ritan's face was twisted in a scowl. His fork was also bent as he gripped it tightly with white knuckles. She could see him struggling to match her actions.

Inwardly, she winced at the punishment that her actions had earned. She had somehow insulted the entire FCM by a simple action of trying to be compassionate.

She ducked her head and grabbed her fork. It was hard eating while standing. The table was a little too low for comfort, but she did the best she could. As they ate, she watched the raptors pick at their food. They didn't seem to eat nearly as much as the humans, though with their size, she couldn't see how they survived.

"Eliza... 73. Why were you in yellow?"

She tensed at the sudden question. The table grew silent in a heartbeat. "I... I'm not sure what you mean."

"I saw you, three of your month ago. You were in eating room. You were in yellow, not in black. Why?"

She didn't know how to answer it. She didn't even knew that he recognized her from her day of reprieve. Helplessly, she looked at Ritan who shook his head sharply with a glare.

Gulping, she looked up at the bright eyes of the raptors looking at her. "I... I had different duties then."

Kraken grunted. He lifted his hand, each claw easily ten centimeters long, and dipped it into a puddle of gravy on his plate. Swirling it around, he lifted his hand up and then began to draw on the table.

When she saw the prisoner insignia being drawn, her breath came faster.

"I not see this symbol on any other crew on your rock. You were in yellow, when everyone wear black and blue and green and dark. You were bright, but now you are dark. From what I see, rank and power is dark on this ship." He finished drawing the prison insignia, including her own serial number. "If you are poisonous, I'm curious what the yellow meant."

Eliza stared down at the image. It was almost perfect with only a few broken lines from where the gravy didn't come off his claw. For his massive body and hand, she saw a precision the Military Intelligence never hinted at. And, at the same time, fear clenched her stomach and turned her dinner to ash.

For all his broken words, she knew that Kraken was far more intelligent than she, or anyone else, realized.

Ritan spoke up. "Ah! How is dinner, Fleet Master?"

Kraken looked up, his blue eyes looking at the colonel across the table. For a painfully long moment, he said nothing.

Eliza grabbed some food to cover her own discomfort.

The raptor barked with laughter. "Cooked and bland and unmoving and as tedious as your presence."

She choked on her food and had to cough to clear her throat. It was going to be a long dinner, but at least she didn't have to explain her prison uniform.

Debriefing

Eliza's heels tapped in rhythm of the heavy thuds of Kraken and the other raptor's paws. It was a staccato sound with a bass beat that sounded like music.

It was a long dinner, filled with uncomfortable silences as Kraken asked pointed questions and forced her and Ritan to answer without revealing everything. Near the end, while Ritan tried to defuse the situation by telling some of the grand tales of the FCM *Quantor's* history, she watched the raptors. Somehow, she got the impression that Kraken was amusing himself more than anything else.

When the dinner ended, Kraken left and Eliza hurried to keep up. Ritan and the others struggled to keep up, but she remained with the aliens instead of her own kind.

"Excuse me, Fleet Master Kraken?"

Kraken continued to walk, but he turned his eye so one eye watched the corridor before them and the other focused on her. It was unnerving to see his intense gaze on her.

"I noticed you didn't seem to enjoy dinner."

"This food is not our own."

"You said unmoving."

He smiled, baring teeth. "Yes, we prefer food that run. Blood that drip from teeth and the squeal of death. Food is more than just fuel, it should be experienced."

She blanched, picturing too well how she thought the alien would eat.

"Your meat." Kraken's voice rumbled and he flicked his tail, "Where does it come from?"

"We grow it, like everything else. Protein slurry and genetic manipulation."

"No wonder you have no life in your kin."

Eliza frowned. "What do you mean?"

Kraken shook his head, still looking in two directions at once. "I try to explain before. Do you think you can understand?"

"I can try."

"Yes, you try. You are," he finished in a guttural language. "I don't know the word."

One of the aides, Gornak, grunted. "Domesticated."

"Yes, domesticated. You have a leash around your neck and all these protocol and procedure. Everything you do follow rule." He waved his paws. "You are trained not to live."

She sighed. "I know." And then she realized she said it out-loud. She looked up guiltily. "Sorry, I didn't mean to say that."

"No, you didn't. You are poorly trained, yes?"

She thought back to the months of heavy labor. She glanced over her shoulder, but none of the other humans were near them. They were struggling to keep up and she realized that somehow she managed to pace the three raptors easily. "Um, I really shouldn't talk about that."

Kraken gestured to the sensor bar, where the light continued to match her movements. "And why do the light follow you?"

Eliza almost choked again. She felt the blood draining from her face and her body shaking. Gulping, she decided to cover up her fear. "Why do you ask these questions?"

"Because I can. Your kind walk on eggshell around me, saying one thing and meaning another. You twist word around to try getting my secret while not revealing your own. It is a hunt, of sort. You attack, I attack, but with word instead of claw and bite."

"And how do we rate, with war of words?"

He barked. "I am glad I finally have an opponent."

Before she could ask, they reached Kraken's wing. It was a cluster of seven quarters, each one larger than her own. She hadn't been inside, but she knew the layout of each one by heart. All seven suites shared a common area, where normally meals would be served.

The door into the common area hissed as it opened.

Kraken looked at her. "You come in?"

"No," gasped Ritan as he hurried to join them. "She has a meeting."

"Ah, pity."

Kraken's tail swung around and slammed against the back of Eliza's leg. The heavy weight staggered her and she stumbled past the door. She braced herself, almost twisting her ankle with her efforts.

Confused, she turned around.

Kraken stuck his head into the common area and looked up above the door. The sensor bar remained lit, the ever-present light indicating she was watched. He grunted and pulled his head back through the door. "Rit-tan 69?"

"Yes?"

"One condition of our quarter here was that we would not be observed."

"We turned off the security system."

"Yes, but our liaison is being watched, yes? Those are camera?"

He paled. "Y-Yes, she has—"

"Our quarter will not be observed. That is the requirement." Kraken's tilted his head and brought it close to Ritan's face. "If she is the liaison, then she must follow the rule like everyone else."

"O-Of course." Ritan's face quickly colored to a ruddy hue. "We will disable the sensor monitoring while she is in your quarters. But, we cannot disable it anywhere else."

"Agreed." Kraken's tail slid back against the wall.

Eliza stared at it for a moment, wondering how much control he had. The intelligence officers didn't mention anything about their control, it was assumed that the tails were only for balance, but Kraken's push felt too deliberate to be an accident.

"Eliza 73, thank you for becoming our liaison. I enjoy your company and your word. I look forward to tomorrow."

She nodded. "Thank you, Fleet Master Kraken. I hope I can serve you to the best of my ability."

Kraken smiled and tilted his head, a gesture Eliza recognized as thinking. He turned back to look at her. "It is good that you are armed. Please remain that way. I feel better with your safety."

Behind her, Ritan inhaled sharply.

She winced at the sound. She assumed that Ritan would have con-fiscated her weapon the second the door shut to the raptor's quar-ters. She looked into Kraken's blue eye, trying to guess the alien's motives.

"I have an opponent," he simply growled before heading into the quarter.

She remained in place as the other two raptors walked past her, each one giving her a deep nod of their head. She bowed back in response, unsure of what it meant.

When the door hissed shut and locked, she remained staring at it for a long moment.

"Captain Midoze 73."

"Yes?" answered Eliza and Duncan.

She turned around, knowing that Ritan was glaring at her.

"My office, now," he snapped.

"Yes, sir."

Duncan spoke up. "What about me?"

"Only her!"

It took them ten minutes to reach his office. Eliza felt the dread gnawing at her gut, but there was nothing she could do. She played through the conversation in her head, seeing things she never no-ticed before from the intelligence reports. She had an idea about giving them a more enjoyable meal, at least, but she wasn't sure if was possible. There was no livestock on the asteroid.

Ritan stormed through the entry room of his office without ac-knowledging his ever-present secretary. The door swung open as he approached, but as soon as he entered his office, he spun around on Eliza. "What the hell are you trying to do?"

She stumbled to a halt. "S-Sir?"

"None of that was on the protocol! You humiliated me in front of those beasts and you know it!"

"I-I—"

"I know what you were doing, Midoze!" Ritan's face purpled as he grabbed her by the front of her uniform and pulled her close. "Listen, this is not a place for your flaws to come out. You are to remain silent and follow the protocols, do you understand? No bringing up questions we don't want answered, no talking about your sentence."

"I didn't!" she snapped back. "He brought it up."

"How did he find out!?"

"You heard him." She gasped as she realized she was screaming at a superior officer. Gulping, she tried to calm herself. "He saw me in the officers dining hall three months ago."

"There is no way he could remember that long ago."

"He did, I swear. You heard everything I said in that dining hall."

"At least until you were running back with him. What were you talking about?"

"Dinner, in specific what he wanted."

"It is perfectly cooked food."

"Yes," she nodded, "perfectly cooked food. Except that they want to chase something living."

Ritan's face twisted into a scowl. "You better be telling the truth."

"Master Colonel Ritan 69, you have me observed every second of my life for the last year and a half. I swear, and you have the recordings to prove it, that I have been honest with you. I am a FCM officer and I will not let my," she snarled, "genetic flaws humiliate my superior officer or my home."

He panted as he glared at her. Then, his fingers creaked as he relaxed and released her. Stepping back, he straightened his outfit and ran his palm through his hair. "Tomorrow, you are not to deviate from your assigned protocols. If the lizard tries to ask personal questions, you are to guide the conversation elsewhere."

"Yes, sir."

"And if the question of your flaws come up in conversation, I want you to lie."

"Then why was I wearing yellow?" She knew it was the wrong thing to say as she opened her mouth, but it was a pointed question by Kraken.

"Just say special services and you aren't authorized to talk about it. Because you are not. If you do, I will throw you out of the airlock myself."

"Yes, sir—"

"Dismissed."

Indecency Violation

Eliza leaned against the wall of the common area and let herself smile. The floor shook from the impact of Kraken landing heavily on the ground, then vaulting over the couch. His tail sailed behind him as he landed easily on the table and raced across it. His passing left deep gouges in the faux wood surface, and he splintered the edge as he jumped across the far end.

A robot scuttled across the ground in front of him. It had a slab of grown meat and dripped synthetic blood in a smear of red behind it. The legs, thick metal, gripped the stone as it dove to the side. The programming was too random, she could tell that, but the raptor seemed to be having fun as he slid against the floor and slammed into the opposing wall with his shoulder.

Kraken roared, and Eliza winced at the powerful noise. Digging deep, he jumped over an upturned couch just as the robot dove underneath it. His clawed feet slammed on the top and the structure cracked from his weight. His head was a blur as he shoved it into the gap.

A crunch of metal signaled the fate of the robot.

Flipping his head up, Kraken tossed the robot in the air and caught it with his teeth. He snarled and shook his head back and forth.

Eliza cringed at the idea of being caught in his grip. Her neck would have been broken by the powerful snaps, something that Kraken explained when she first proposed the idea of the robot meal.

Sitting down heavily, Kraken brought his tail up. He levered it into the space between the inedible robot and the hunk of meat. With a twist, he tore the two apart and noisily ate the meat.

The robot crashed into the ground, sparks flying and one leg quivering. Oil spread out from the carcass, mixing with the blood that pooled around it.

In the door of two of the suites, the other raptors watched. Both were quivering, their version of excitement, and long streamers of drool dripped from their mouths.

A rumble shook the air as Kraken started to purr. It sounded like a buzz saw as he finished tearing apart his meal and swallowed it. "Yes, yes."

She felt a glow of excitement. "How was your meal?"

He looked at her. "The best in many month."

"Please," asked Gornak. "I go next?"

Hissa ducked her head and stepped back. It was a sign of submission and agreement. Since Eliza's started to report her observations, the military intelligence learned more than ever about the social aspects of raptor society.

Kraken nodded and stood up. He thumped across the room, blood dribbling down the side of his jaw, and into the room with the rest of dinner. They didn't have enough for a large prey robot, nor the room, but Eliza guessed if they had an active appetizer, unmoving fake bloody meat would be still be satisfying. The raptors agreed to try it, and it already looked like a success.

She reached down and pulled out the second robot. They were all prototypes, but the steaming meat was already dripping blood on her hands and staining her uniform. She looked up at Gornak who shook with excitement.

With a grin, she activated the robot and let it go.

Gornak squealed and launched himself after the robot.

Eliza stepped back into the suite the raptors used for paperwork. She looked at her hands and sighed. She would be reported for her stained uniform, but she could at least clean up. She knew it was sterile, the blood was as fake as the meat, but that didn't help with the idea she had blood on her hands.

She headed straight for the bathroom. The raptors didn't use it, so she picked it as her personal spot while she spent time in the raptor suites. Closing the door, she scrubbed her hands clean and promised herself to grab a pair of gloves for next time.

Even through the heavy walls, she could hear Gornak chasing after his meal and Hissa barking.

After she finished scrubbing, she used the bathroom. But, as she was fastening her uniform, she caught sight of a blood on her stomach. Somehow, she missed a spot on her hand. Beneath the smear of crimson was her scarred belly, the thin lines of her prison sentence still a map against her pale skin.

She stood there, staring at her body. She spent so long trying not to think about it and, in a moment of weakness, she saw herself as she used to. She was beautiful, not that anyone cared anymore. With a whimper, she tried to tear her thoughts away from the dark place but she couldn't. All she could see were nipples standing up and begging to be touched. Or the dusting of pubic hair that did little to hide the curve of her sex.

Tears burned in her eyes. She gripped her uniform shut and wiped her eyes with her other hand. She sniffed and closed her eyes tightly, unwilling to torture herself by reminding of what she had lost.

But, as she opened her eyes, she found herself looking up at the dark sensor bar. The ever-present light was gone in the raptor's suites, even in the bathroom. She was pretty sure they couldn't activate the sensors without the light, that was part of the Accountability Protocol every child was taught at an early age.

An idea, a shameful one, bubbled up. She shook as she pulled open her uniform again, looking down at her bare breasts and her naked skin. She could feel a heat rising up inside her as she considered risking everything for a flawed craving.

"No," she gasped and clutched her uniform close. Turning around, she sat heavily on the toilet. Her hand shook as she held it in place, terrified at how fast her willpower was crumbling.

Tears trailed the line of her curve. She took in a deep breath, shuddering as she did. As she exhaled, she slid her foot to the side, spreading her thighs and leaning back.

She sobbed and winced at how it echoed against the walls. Looking at the door, the fear of being caught slammed into her. She released her uniform to bite down on the side of her palm to silence herself. With her other hand, she pulled the uniform off her breasts and brought her palm to the hot bump of her nipple.

More tears rolled down her cheeks as she stroked her nipple in a circle, enjoying every forbidden surge of pleasure as she explored the once familiar crinkle of her areola and the hardness that tugged at her skin. Her scars added texture to her touch and she felt the heat building quickly from the unfamiliarity.

She had forgotten her own body in the last year. It felt like she was touching a stranger, not that she would ever know.

Eliza caught her nipple with her hand and tweaked it. Her nipples and clitoris were connected and both throbbed with the sensations. Deep inside, her pussy muscles clenched at the bolt of pleasure. Gasping, she twisted it again, enjoying the discomfort and pleasure that rocketed along her nerves.

She bit down harder on her palm as she rubbed her nipple. Her breath came in gasps. It tickled the back of her hand and added to the sparkle of pain from the teeth digging into her skin. But, she kept stroking and squeezing.

In seconds, her pussy grew slick and wet. She could smell her excitement drifting up around her, flooding her senses with the almost familiar scent of pleasure. She kept squeezing and relaxing her inner muscles, trying to imagine what it would feel like to have something other than her fingers or a brush inside her.

Moments later, her nipples weren't enough. Moaning into her palm, she slid her hand down the ribbed surface of her belly. She forgot about the blood and it left a smear of crimson across her skin, but she didn't care. It was sterile and slick.

She almost came at the sensation of her fingertips sliding over her pubic mound. She blindly traced the swollen folds of her sex. The heated slickness, she remembered that, but not the caress of her fingers against her aching clitoris.

Moaning, she bit down harder and shoved her fingertips against her clitoris and began to stroke it in small circles. Each touch ripped a gasp out of her and she strained to spread her legs further apart while rubbing faster. Her fingers quickly grew slick and dripping, but she didn't care. The patter of her juices dripping into the toilet only added to the gasping moans that filled the tiny bathroom.

After so long without an orgasm, she forgot what it felt like to have that growing sense of pleasure swelling up inside her. It was hot and slick. Her chest hurt and her body trembled as it spread out to fill her body. Every cell of her body seemed to quiver as she rubbed faster.

The wet slurps of her fingers echoed against the walls, barely audible over her gasps. She ground her teeth against her palm. She tasted blood in her mouth, but didn't care.

She picked herself up from the toilet, her back arching to use the wall for balance. Her fingers moved furiously as she strained to reach a shameful orgasm.

And then it slammed into her. One moment, she felt it rising into a crest that thought would never pass. And in the next, she was kneeling on the bathroom floor, pumping two fingers furiously into her cunt as stars exploded across her vision. Her orgasm tore through her and briefly shredded her sanity. She could only sob as she brutally violated herself until her world was nothing but her burning pussy, pleasure, and pain.

The white-hot intensity seared her senses and then she lost all tension. With a groan, she slumped to the ground, heedless as her head thumped against the wall. The after-tremors of her orgasm spasmed her muscles and she gasped for breath, trying to clear her mind.

And then the pleasure faded as she realized that she may have just sentenced herself to life in prison. She curled up and sobbed, cursing her inability to control herself. She was flawed. Utterly and completely broken, a throwback to cruder times. She didn't deserve to live anymore.

Sniffing, she forced herself to her feet. Using a washcloth, she cleaned the blood and her juices from her body with simple functional wipes. She promised she would never break down again as she fastened her uniform.

When she went to open the bathroom door, she caught sight of her hand. There was an indention of her teeth in a perfect circle. Blood welled up from the imprint of her incisors, the shallow cuts only a scrape. She sighed and closed her eyes.

Eliza couldn't do it anymore. She was flawed. A long time ago, Ritan authorized her to take a long walk from an airlock. She tapped her wrist and scrolled through the memory. Her archives were very short with her prison sentence, but she found it. She was still authorized to access the airlocks.

Wiping the tears from her face, she took a deep breath. She could do it. She could serve the greater good one last time. She just needed Kraken to give her a little time to finish the deed before she lost her courage.

It took her another breath before she could open the bathroom door. Padding out, she saw the carcasses of three robots strewn across the room. Either Hissa or Gornak had torn theirs apart completely and the parts were scattered everywhere.

She felt broken as she walked into the other room. The three raptors were tearing into the pile of synthetic meat. Blood coated the walls and pooled on the ground. Clawed paw prints circled the room as the three aliens growled at each other while tearing apart their food with claw, teeth, and tail.

Suddenly, all three stopped. She felt a prickle of sensation as their tails rose up, circling toward their heads.

Kraken lifted his head, blood coating his face, and looked at her.

"Um, Fleet Master Kraken? Do you mind if I do something? It won't take long." She almost sobbed but fought it back to hide her intentions.

"No."

"I... what?"

Kraken tilted his head to stare at her with one eye. "I use wrong word? Negative? Disagreement? Permission denied?"

As he spoke, Gornak and Hissa sniffed the air, their heads rocking back and forth. It was as if the bloody meal was suddenly not important.

She gulped. "I mean, why not?"

Kraken stepped over the blood strewn remains of a couch. His clawed footprints squelched on the ground. He padded over to her and she lifted her head to look up into his bright blue eyes. He leaned down to her and sniffed.

She shivered, wondering if he could somehow tell that she had just ruined everything. Or that he could see her flaw.

Kraken's eyes never left her as he lowered his head even further, until his nose was even with her breasts. With his nose resting against her stomach, he sniffed loudly.

A whimper rose up in her throat.

He tilted his head and lowered even further, his massive body somehow lowering down as he brought his head even with her hips.

She inhaled sharply, staring down at the bright red head that was centimeters away from her sex. He knew what she had done, she knew it. Tears welled up in her eyes as she stared down into the bright blue eyes. Inside, she clenched her inner muscles with anticipation.

Kraken didn't sniff. Instead, he sharply lifted his head and peered at her.

Eliza sniffed and tried to resist the tears. "I-I'm sorry."

"For what, Eliza Midoze 73?"

"I... I'm flawed."

"Really."

It took her a moment to realize he didn't ask a question. "I am."

"How so?"

The tears came rolling down her face. She shook her head, unable to find the words.

Kraken licked the tears from her face. His rough tongue stunk of meat and blood, but there was something intimate about his action that stole her breath away. She could hear him purring, a deep rumbling noise in his thick chest.

He pulled back. "You smell good."

She opened her mouth, then closed it. After a second, she tried again. "I what?"

With a smile, Kraken bobbed his head. "You smell good now. This smell, I like."

"Oh." She glanced down and saw her hand. She lifted it up to him. "I hurt myself."

Kraken said nothing, but his tail continued to sweep back and forth.

A blush burned on Eliza's cheeks. "I... damn it. You can smell it?"

"Yes." He smiled as his tail curled up. "It smells like life."

"Life? No, I'm flawed. I can't—"

"What, live? Spar with word? Show understanding of my kind? Have compassion? Think for yourself?"

"No... I mean, yes, but."

He lifted his head before he shook it. "No, you may not leave. I do not trust you not to hurt yourself. You stay here."

She clutched herself and nodded. "I can stay until later."

Kraken leaned forward to rest his nose against her cheek. "I meant, move your home."

"W-What?" The world spun around her.

"You fear the recording and sensor strip. I see it in your body, your language. You may not have a tail, but you human are just as easy to read. You are flawed, yes, in the eye of the other human, but you are the only one not flawed in our eye."

Eliza glanced at the other raptors who bobbed their heads. She gulped. "I-I can't ask for that. They won't let me do that."

Kraken laughed. "I did not say ask. I said move. I will deal with Ritan."

Eliza nodded, her heart pounding in her chest and her world torn apart. She felt naked and free, but terrified at the same time. "O-Okay."

He nodded and headed back to his meal.

She stepped back, then stopped in shock. "You just said Ritan, not Rit-tan."

Kraken looked over his shoulder as his tail swept back and forth. "Did I? No, I am sure I said Rit-tan."

Self-Pleasuring 10

Eliza woke up without knowing where she was. She could smell her body on the pillows, but the blankets were softer than she ever remembered. With a moan, she stretched out before she remembered the sensors. She gasped and curled up into a fetal position before she peered out of the blankets. Her eyes focused on the sensor strip, looking for the light that indicated the ever-present recordings.

The strip she saw was dark. Her mind still struggling with her surroundings, she lifted herself and peered around the room. All of the strips were dark.

And then she remembered. She had moved to the raptor's quarters the night before. Ritan had signed the order reluctantly after Kraken toyed with him in a crowded dinner among the ship's superior officers. She remembered seeing the Chief Master Colonel smirking behind a napkin on one occasion as Ritan struggled with an obviously superior opponent.

She grinned at Ritan's final humiliation when Kraken suggested that Eliza move to his quarters, to "make it easier to perform her duties" during Kraken's inconsistent schedule. At that point, there was no other answer than a sullen agreement.

Warmed by the memory of Ritan's defeat, she slipped out of the bed. Her sleeping outfit, almost a uniform itself, rustled with her movements. She straightened it to avoid it riding up and padded into the bathroom.

She started the steam shower and slipped off her clothes. She avoided looking at herself in the mirror before stepping into the column of heated water. The heat and moisture felt good rolling along her skin. Unlike the prison, there was no countdown for her shower and she intended to remain in the water until her skin wrinkled.

Tilting her head up, she combed her fingers through her short hair and scrubbed her scalp. The soap bubbled around her fingers before dribbling down over her sensitive skin. As much as she resisted, she couldn't help but concentrate on the feeling of the water sheeting down her stomach to tickle along the sensitive folds of her labia.

She finished cleaning her hair and moved to her face. Scrubbing briskly, she let the steam rinse it clean.

And then she saw Kraken's head sticking through the bathroom door.

Eliza did a double take and then scrambled back, pressing her hand over her breast and crotch. "Kraken!"

He barked out a laugh. "You look happy in that moment." His rumbling voice boomed in the tiny confines of the bathroom.

"I was!" She took a deep breath. "I was."

"I know, I enjoyed watching you."

She blushed, her hand over her breasts wavering. "Y-You did? Why?"

He tilted his head and stepped further into the room. His bulk didn't fit, but he managed to pry enough of his body to loom over her. "Many reasons," he said with a rumbling chuckle. "Curiosity, of course, but curious about many thing."

Eliza found her breath coming faster. "What kind of things?"

"What you look like under your uniform for starters." He grinned. "And what you do when no one is watching."

A heat tickled her skin. She curled her fingers against her pussy, clamping her palm against her sex to protected it. Despite her efforts, she brought her fingers to the rapidly heating folds of her labia.

She cleared her throat, berating herself for her thoughts, but didn't move her hand. "You... you wanted to see me touch myself."

Kraken tilted his head. "Yes, and I am enjoying that you are doing that." He gestured to her hand.

Eliza realized what she was doing. She was fingering herself, the digits already passed the outer folds of her sex. She blushed and forced her hand away. A moment later, she realized he could already see her most private of places and lowered her other hand to reveal her pert nipples to the raptor's eye.

As the steam rolled down her body, she stood there naked. Her heart thumped as she stared at the raptor, silently daring him to say anything. When he didn't, she slowly turned around to give him a good view. As she finished coming around, she blushed even hotter as her boldness.

"Yes, an enjoyable view." Kraken bowed his head. "Thank you, Eliza. I am grateful."

He pulled out.

Eliza watched him and, for a strange reason, felt a longing for his company. There was something about his words, the way he made her feel. She spread her fingers through the steam and watched it pour through the gaps. With a deep breath, she called out to him. "Kraken? Are you there?"

"Yes."

She bit her lower lip before she stepped out of the steam. Behind her, the vents silenced and she walked, dripping and barefoot, to the door and peered outside while using the frame to shield herself.

Kraken filled the other end of the bedroom. His bulk reached almost to the ceiling and the bright red of his skin looked almost like fire. He wasn't wearing his normal harness and she could see the bright yellow stripes almost reached his belly. His tail curled up his body, almost touching his head.

She felt a rush of excitement. "A-Aren't you still curious?"

He bobbed his head. "Yes, but it would be inappropriate for my move. You know my intent."

She hesitated at his use of "move," it sounded like a game. Pushing it aside, she gave a hesitant smile. "But, you still want to see?"

He smiled and turned toward her. "Of course."

"Why?"

"As I said, curious. It is the nature of all intelligent thing."

She clutched the door frame. "They don't encourage curiosity here."

"I did say 'intelligent.'" His tail twitched.

She gave a hesitant smile. "I didn't think being a pervert was intelligence."

Kraken laughed, his booming bark echoing against the walls. "Perversion is the ultimate curiosity. All intelligent creature look at something and wonder if it can be eaten, drunk, smoked, or..." He titled his head more, "fucked."

A heat bubbled up along her body. She giggled at his words and nervously at her own thoughts before she stepped out from behind the door. Without even the thin veil of steam from her shower, she felt naked and vulnerable to the brightly colored alien in front of her.

He stepped closer, his tail rising to the ceiling. She could hear his breath, a deep rumble that shook the air as he purred.

Blood rushing in her ears, she stepped into the middle of the room.

His paws thudded on the ground as he circled around her, inspecting her with one eye and then the other. Then, he stopped and crouched in front of her. With one claw, he reached up and cupped her chin, tilted her head to look up at him.

She trembled, knowing that it would take only a swipe to rip her throat out. Her body burned with humiliation, excitement, and anticipation.

He drew close until his nose pressed against her cheek. The coolness of his body was a contrast to her own warmth. When he exhaled, she felt it tickle her ear and hair. "Eliza."

Up close, his voice shook her, and she moaned.

"I admit. I am still curious."

"A-About what?" Her throat was tight. Her nipples ached to be touched. Among the smells of the shower and soap, she caught a whiff of her own pussy growing excited.

"How you make yourself smell good."

Between her legs, she felt his tail touch her inner thigh. Her entire body tensed up at the caress. It was sure and delicate, not clumsy like she expected. He teased her calf, swirling up through the water and soap clinging to her body.

Whimpering, she looked up at him. It was wrong. He was an alien and she knew nothing about him.

When the tip of his tail caressed her knee, she stumbled back. "No."

Kraken bobbed his head. "Very well, I will stop."

Still blushing, she shook her head. "No, I mean that wasn't it. I..." She gulped. "I used my fingers."

"Really."

She nodded. "Do you..." She had to take a deep breath. "Want to see?"

He turned his head so he was looking at her with his other eye. "No."

"No?" She tensed.

"I rather see you on that bed and relaxed then frantic on a toilet. I want you to enjoy showing me. To know what curiosity feels like."

Her knees buckled for a moment, and she clutched his side. His was huge against her, a giant to her smallness, but he was more compassionate than any human she had ever known.

"Would you do this for me, Eliza?"

"Y-Yes, I would."

"I would be grateful."

Trembling with anticipation, she pushed herself away from Kraken and walked backwards to her bed. She stared into his eye, basking in her vulnerability but also in the submission to his desires.

At the edge, she sat down. With her hands, she pried her thighs apart, fighting her internal reluctance as much as swimming in the heady rush of doing the forbidden. If anyone caught her, she would be executed by the end of the hour. Somehow, that made the inferno inside her only burn hotter.

"Hissa guard the door, no one will interrupt."

She let out a little giggle. "You planned this."

He said nothing, but his tail swept back and forth before curling back over his head.

"All for this?" She arched her back and brought one hand between her legs. She worked her digits in the slick folds and spread herself open. The cool air caressed her clitoris and along the sensitive skin, adding to her rapidly growing pleasure.

Kraken's breath came in deep purrs. He crouched and lowered his head, bobbing as he kept one eye locked on her sex.

She used her middle finger to circle around her clitoris, teasing the fold of pleasure until it ached. When she couldn't take it anymore, she dragged her fingernails along the length of her labia and teased herself open. Arching her back, she delved her fingers into her hole.

Whimpers filled her bedroom as she pumped her fingers into her sex, sliding them deep before drawing them out. She held up her fingers and showed Kraken the clear liquid rolling down her digits.

His purring grew louder.

"Any other questions?"

He lifted his gaze. "You are not done."

"No, but you are purring rather loudly." She grinned. "I thought you were... curious."

A chuckle. "Yes. I am."

She bit her lip and flipped her hand over to let her juices dribbling down the other side. "What are you curious about?"

Kraken turned his head to look at her with his other eye. "Are you sure you want to know? Curiosity is a drug."

She lowered her hand to her pussy, stroking her clitoris with her palm. She smiled and nodded.

"Have you tasted yourself?"

She froze. "I... I never thought to try."

His tail swept back and forth.

Eliza bent herself to give her more access. The heat of her own sex seared her fingertips as she drove three fingers deep into her body, pumping until the room echoed with the wet slurps of her excitement. Her moans, guttural and desperate, rose as she felt her orgasm swelling up inside her.

She focused on Kraken, staring into his eyes as her movements grew more frantic. The wet pumping drove bolts of pleasure through her veins and she saw sparks.

Across her sweat and water-slicked body, she saw that Kraken's was also responding to her. A long bulge had formed between his legs. It looked like a rod swelling just underneath his skin.

She flushed at the realization he was turned on by her actions. It drove her to pump faster and harder, pumping her fingers deep until her pleasure curled her toes.

Her orgasm tore through her and she screamed shrilly. Her entire body tensed until her muscles screamed out in agony. She arched completely off the bed, one foot braced on the edge and her head holding her up as she strained to keep pumping, but she couldn't get purchase.

Instead, she remained frozen as her world exploded into flames and then snuffed out almost instantly. Her body grew slack and she thumped to her bed. With a moan, she slipped off the bed and struck the ground.

Panting, she looked up at the raptor towering above her. He was excited, she knew that, judging from the thick pole straining along his crotch. It was a sheath of some sort, but he wasn't erect enough for it to slide out. She forced her eyes up at him and gave a soft, gasping chuckle.

"I enjoyed that," Kraken said in a throaty growl.

"I've never done that before. I mean, no one has ever seen me do that."

"A pity; it was beautiful."

She had to lift her hips to pull her fingers from her sex. She was dripping as she admired her fingers. Slowly, she looked back up to see Kraken panting heavily ahead of her.

Trembling, she stared into his eye as she brought her fingers to her mouth. The smell of her pussy was strong and the heat tickled her senses, but she dipped her fingers into her mouth.

She came again, a tiny orgasm rippling through her body. Her pussy spasmed at the taste of her sex, her forbidden actions adding to her pleasure. She panted and she sucked her finger, cleaning each one until her digits glistened with her saliva.

Between his legs, Kraken's cock finally pushed out of his sheath. As the slit swelled open, it looked like a red rod was moving out of his body. The tip was a blunted arrow. It didn't have a ridge or glans, just a spear tip that already dripped clear liquid.

She reached out for it, unsure of her actions, but he pulled back. Only a few centimeters had pushed out of his sheath, but it bobbed stiffly with his movement. In the air, she could pick up a sharp, musky scent that swirled around her.

Kraken pulled back and turned away.

Trembling, she looked up.

He cleared his throat. He was shaking himself, a violet spasm that coursed along his massive length. He padded for the door.

"Kraken? Did I do something wrong?"

Kraken stopped the door and peered at her with one blue eye. "That is not the move for now. I still have secret."

She waited for more, but he didn't speak. She nodded and leaned against the bed. "T-Thank you."

"For what, Eliza?"

"Making me feel good."

"You did the same for me. I am thankful for sating my curiosity." He bowed his head and walked out, the ground thudding with every step.

And then, as he left the room, she heard his final words.

"For now."

Her First Lessons

Eliza stood at attention on the landing docking of the hanger. Her arm ached from holding her palm to the side of her head. She could feel it along her shoulder and back. Her position allowed for no movement but she doggedly struggled to remain in position until Ritan ordered the "at ease."

An hour ago, the raptor transport flight was supposed to land. The announcement came in and Ritan made the order to present. She was the only inferior officer on the platform besides the raptors, and she obeyed immediately. But, then procedures prevented the ship from landing and he never gave the order to relax.

She stared at the ship hovering meters away from the platform. Unlike the black ships of the FCM, the raptor ships were brightly colored with organic patterns along their surface. Kraken said that the colors identified the various squadrons of fighters and transports, typically matching the coloration of the primary pilot for each ship. The one in front of her was blue with yellow blotches along the belly. It was a Bronto-class Transport Freighter. From her vantage point, she thought it looked like some pregnant lizard with a swollen belly.

Glancing to the side, she saw Ritan standing two meters away at ease. There was a cruel smile on his face, and she was sickened by the sight of his pettiness.

Kraken called it a fight, but with words instead of claws. She felt like a pawn between the two males, but it was obvious that she trusted the raptor far more than the man who tried to have her executed. She hated the man and her hatred only grew with each jab he inflicted on her because he couldn't win against Kraken.

As her thoughts turned to the raptor, she glanced to the other side. Kraken, Hissa, and Gornak stood along the shipping boxes of their quarters. The fleet master seemed amused with his tail swinging back and forth. She could feel the thump as it struck one of the boxes or bumped against Gornak's paws. Occasionally, Hissa or Gornak would try to stomp Kraken's tail and he would jerk it out of the way. After weeks of watching them, she realized they were playing.

She was only beginning understand the game Kraken played. There was nothing he could do to force Ritan to release her and both of them knew it. She was also not in a position to drop her posture, and that only added to her growing hatred of Ritan and everything he represented.

Time stretched out and Eliza felt the muscles in her back protesting. It was one thing to swing a hammer for hours at a time, it was a far different to remain still for an hour at a time. She prayed that one of the men would do something to relieve her.

The hovering ship engine suddenly roared. The rockets flared brilliantly, and the craft surged forward. It came up over the edge of the platform before slamming heavily down on the platform. The impact of the gigagrams of weight shook the platform, sending boxes cascading everywhere and Ritan and Eliza sprawling.

Ritan surged back to his feet, his face red. "They aren't authorized to land!"

Kraken stepped over Eliza as he padded over to Ritan. "Pilot allow to land when low on fuel. She must have run out, Rit-tan." As he spoke, his tail swept back and forth with his amusement.

Ritan glared at the raptor and then to Eliza who was getting back to her feet.

She wondered if Ritan would order her back into position, but she saw the colonel sigh with annoyance. With a thrill, she stood up and rubbed her aching shoulder.

Instead, he turned back to Kraken. "Inspections must have taken longer than normal."

"No doubt. She is a very big ship with many supply for your home. I can see why you want to inspect. Have guards protect entrance and finish without wasting our limited fuel."

Ritan's jaw clenched. He shook his head. "No, I'm sure their inspections were sufficient. I wouldn't want to hinder your return back to the fleet."

Kraken bowed his head and held out one clawed hand. "Thank you. Rit-tan, it is a pleasure to interact with you again. May you have safety until we return in one month."

"I can't wait," Ritan said through clenched teeth.

"Do not worry, your spy shall give you many reports—"

"She isn't a spy!"

"Really." Kraken turned and headed toward the platform that opened up from the jaw of the ship. His tail swept around, smacking Ritan in the shin before he passed.

Hissa and Gornak followed after him. Their tails swung back and forth and Ritan staggered back to avoid being struck again.

Various crew started to gather up the spilled boxes and loaded them onto carts before pushing them toward the ship. At the same time, more crew started to unload the loaded craft. The fleet's boxes were wooden, to her surprise, but marked with insignias from various FCM divisions. She spotted ones for the food, technology, and entertainment divisions. Almost half of the boxes were assigned to the various military branches.

Eliza gathered up her personal pack, hoisted it over her shoulder, and started after Kraken. The heels of her formal outfit tapped against the ground in a staccato rhythm barely audible over the din of moving carts.

Ritan stopped her as she passed. "Captain Midoze 73."

She saluted. "Yes, sir?"

He leaned into her. "It would give me great pleasure to find that you were torn apart and slaughtered on that ship."

The muscles of her check and legs tightened. "Y-Yes, sir."

"Until then, remember your duties."

She straightened her back and held her salute. "Yes, sir."

Ritan turned and stormed off.

Eliza held her salute for a long count. She watched the colonel leave the hanger, and a bitter anger simmered inside her. The muscles in her jaw tightened and her teeth ground together. As soon as Ritan walked out of sight, she released her salute and stepped back.

Turning on her heels, she marched into the maw of the alien ship.

Kraken waited for her at the top of the ramp.

She snarled at him. "Why didn't you do anything?"

He bobbed his head and laughed. "It was not my move."

Eliza slowed to a stop and stared. "W-Who's move was it? Was it Ritan's?"

He smiled, baring his sharp teeth. Stepping up to her, he lowered his head to her level.

She stared at him, her heart thumping loudly.

Without a word, Kraken pressed his nose against her cheek.

For a long moment, neither moved. Eliza panted underneath her breath, his touch was intimate and delicate, a stark contrast to his size and strength.

He pulled back and turned away. "The pilot does not have a secondary. If you wish to see how our ships fly, I recommend you join her."

Her jaw opened and her bag slipped from her shoulder. It hit the ground with a thud. "Me?"

"Of course. Very sad that her secondary got sick. Violation of protocol to only have one pilot on ship."

A flash of insight blossomed across her thoughts. She snapped her mouth shut and glared at him. "Damn it! You're manipulating me!"

Kraken looked over his shoulder at her, his tail curling up at the end. "Really."

Eliza watched as the raptor headed down the wide corridor. The walls were painted brightly, all in blues and yellows. She spotted murals among the colors, pictures of what looked like family and growing up. Curious, she followed after him at a slower pace, looking at the images as she passed.

It took her a few minutes to navigate her way to the cockpit. The broad display caught her attention; it was larger than the room she had as a lieutenant. Two seats sat next to each other, but they were smaller than she expected.

"Hello! You be Liz?" A child's voice filled the cockpit.

Eliza spotted the speaker after a second, a tiny blue crested head peeking over the seat. It wasn't a raptor, at least one not like the ones she knew. Her head was smaller than Eliza's fist. Tiny claws, no larger than Eliza's finger, clutched the side.

"Hi! I'm Billie!" The alien jumped up on the back of the seat. She was barely a meter long, a miniature raptor with smaller teeth, a narrower head, and longer tail.

Eliza hesitantly stepped forward. "I'm Major Captain Eliza Midoze 73."

"I'm... Billie." The alien turned her head, peering at Eliza with a bright yellow eye. Her coloration matched the ship almost perfectly, with an even azure across the top of her body and yellow splotches on her belly. She wore no harness but she had a ring piercing the tip of her tail and another at her throat.

Blushing, Eliza peered at the other seat. It looked large enough for herself.

"Wow, you are pretty."

Eliza smiled. "So are you."

Billie trilled, a flutter of skin rippling along her neck.

"Can I call you Liz? Hard to say long name but I know you human like formal name. And strange number at the end."

"It's a generation number. But, Liz is okay."

"Generation? What about your mommy?" The little raptor peered at her. "Are you an orphan?"

Eliza smiled and sank into the chair. It was soft and cushioned, but not smooth. The faint texture teased her thighs as she settled into place. A fruity smell rose up around her, surrounding her in perfume. "No, I don't have parents. We were conceived in tubes. My batch is 75% of the Midoze genetic material with 25% from the Gorfin 2 line."

Billie sank into her seat. Her long tail curled around her and she let out a soft trill. "Sounds kind of boring."

"Yeah."

"Well, you won't be bored on Krak's ship."

Eliza felt a shiver of anticipation. "I hope so."

"Maybe you find some time and meet my baby and husband?"

She looked up at her. Billie looked tiny, a child at the earliest.

Billie trilled again. "Ah, Liz not know about the fleet. Oh, yeah. The other spy get killed before reporting back. But, you will not. Billie take care of you."

Stunned, Eliza could only nod.

"Good. My family like you for dinner." Billie licked her lips as she pulled a miniature control panel into her lap. Grabbing a flight stick with one hand and her other claw along buttons, she tapped a few buttons and the ship began to rumble.

A prickle of fear tingled along Eliza. "Dinner?"

Another trill and a bob of her head. "Do not worry. You too big to eat, all that meat spoil. And then Krak get angry and everyone die. So, eat food with family instead and talk."

Eliza felt her heart thump at the little creature's words. She turned and stared at the control panel, but she didn't recognize the layout or even the symbols. She knew the raptors had their own language, but military intelligence said it wasn't important. Now, as she stared at a controls in a language she didn't know, she wished she spent at least a little time learning Kraken's language.

"You press the magnetic release?"

Eliza looked at Billie helplessly. "I-I don't know what to press. I don't know your language. I-I'm sorry."

Billie pushed her controls away. She jumped up to her feet, then hopped over to Eliza. Before Eliza could pull back, Billie peered up at her face with one yellow eye. "We learn your language. Why not you?"

In response, Eliza had to look away. "We weren't told to."

"Did you want to?"

Eliza looked into the piercing yellow eyes of the alien peering over her. She gulped and then nodded.

"Good! I teach you." Billie jumped on Eliza's lap. Her claws pierced the fabric of Eliza's skirt, but it was tiny pricks instead of slashes. Turning three times, she curled into a ball in Eliza's lap.

Eliza giggled nervously at the raptor on her thighs.

Billie curled her tail around her and peeked up at the controls. "Okay, start with the magnetic release. It says 'magnetic' and it is right there." She tapped a button with her tail.

Hesitantly, Eliza reached over and pressed the button. It had a satisfying thunk as it depressed. The ship also shuddered with the familiar sensation of the clamps disengaging.

"Now, push the control release." The narrow blue tail pointed to a button. "That says 'release'."

Staring at the symbols for a moment, Eliza pressed it. As the ship began to rise, she reflexively grabbed the stick and rested her hand on the keyboard, just like she always did in her own ship.

"You flew before?"

"Yes, a fighter."

"Lots of guns?"

"Four plasma cannons and a missile launcher. With a small rail gun for backup."

"This baby," Billie tapped the side of the chair, "only has a single cannon. So, just pretend it is a large fighter?"

Eliza smiled and nodded. "I can do that."

Billie trilled with approval and twisted against Eliza's lap. Her tail tickled Eliza's wrist as she pointed to the next button. "Now press the igniter."

12 Opening Up

Billie never moved from her lap, cheerfully talking about her family while identifying buttons when Eliza got stuck. It took Eliza a while to realize that even though none of the raptors spoke with plurals, the tiny creature had hundreds, if not thousands, of children. But, even the idea of so many children didn't detract from the alien lizard's cheerful manner or playfulness.

Like Kraken, Billie was curious and probed Eliza for information, but Billie's questions were tactless and blunt compared to Kraken's delicate twists.

Eliza defended herself as well as she could, though she occasionally snapped louder than she thought.

Billie didn't appear to mind and simply changed the topic. Her cheerful manner never wavered nor did her lessons on the ship. The labels were foreign, but a spaceship was a spaceship. The basics of how to navigate and dock were unchanged in a thousand years and the shared skilled between raptor and human bridged the gap.

Distracted by her lessons, Eliza's first sight of the raptor fleet came when she wasn't expecting it. A flash on the control panel caught her attention. "What's that?"

"Oh, the fleet." Billie reached up to tap a few buttons with her tail. "That would be the nest ship, our home."

The screen flashed and zoomed on the ships. At first, she only saw a yellow-striped red ship. It looked like a large egg with the same colors as Kraken. The screen continued to zoom in until the egg ship filled the screen. Eliza spotted little spots near the middle of the egg. The computer continued to zoom in until the spots became a fleet of ships, all of them shaped like eggs or lizards or birds.

Eliza stared in shock. "How big is that red one?"

"About a tenth the size of your asteroid."

"All those other ships looked like they can fit inside."

"They do, when we jump. Otherwise, we sail out to explore. We all need space when we are not jumping."

Eliza sighed and patted Billie on the head.

The little blue lizard started to purr and leaned into her palm.

"What is there to explore out here? I've never seen anything."

Billie flexed her claws against Eliza's thigh. "You never know. The last jump brought us into an asteroid belt. There was a lot of screeching until we got out, but then we spend many month mining and building. It be a good time."

"Didn't you know you were going into an asteroid belt?"

"No," purred Billie. "Every jump is random. They end up near large gravity well, like your asteroid, but other than that, all surprise."

"Aren't you afraid of dying?"

"Yes."

Eliza frowned. "Why do you do it then?"

Billie lifted her head to peer at Eliza. "Would you want to spend your life just sailing through the dark?"

With a sigh, Eliza rested her hand on Billie's warm body and held the control. She thought about the endless patrols and the pseudo-randomness of her waypoints. It wasn't any different than the strict schedule of the prison levels.

Billie's claws on her chin broke Eliza from her thoughts. Eliza gasped and looked down.

"Do not you worry. The fleet be fun for you. Little Billie take care of Liz. I will not let anyone eat you."

"Um, thanks."

13 Opponents

Eliza thought her eyes were going to pop out of her head. The tunnels of the nest ship were completely different than anything she had seen before. Instead of military crew walking in silence wearing dark outfits, there wasn't anything less than brilliantly colored. Hundreds, if not thousands, of raptors and other lizard-like creatures ran everywhere. She saw ones smaller than Billie and quadrupeds easily three times larger than Kraken.

And the noise. The screeches, trills, and screams beat against the walls. She heard little raptors screeching with ear-piercing volume and the low growl of the larger creatures. She could hear them speaking, but the guttural words were still foreign. Wishing she could understand, she thought about asking Billie for more lessons.

The other thing she noticed were the chambers. Large hallways interrupted the tunnels at random intervals. They were filled with platforms and fountains, brightly colored trees and yet more lizard-like aliens. They passed through a market of some sort, as least she thought it was a market. The socialistic nature of the FCM *Quantor* meant supplies were provided on request and rationing. But, with the raptors, she saw rings being passed in exchange for a dizzying array of foods, clothing, and tools. Her stomach rumbled as she tried to identify the smells.

Eliza realized she was trailing behind Kraken and hurried up. She had to run the last few meters before matching his pace.

He looked at her with his bright blue eye. "Overwhelming?"

"A little..." She decided to be more honest. "Yes."

"Do not worry. A hot bath will help you relax. Maybe you will only see things you have already seen."

She glanced at him and felt a blush rising on her cheeks.

Kraken chuckled. His tail swung around to wrap around her waist. With a sharp pull, he dragged her closer. His nose rested on her cheek for a moment before he pulled back.

Eliza gasped and stumbled closer to him. She planted a hand against his side to avoid falling. His chuckle vibrated her palm and her cheeks burned with his closeness.

She walked in silence, shielding herself with Kraken's body and staring out at the wondrous places they passed. The colors and noises were becoming disquieting. She turned and stared at Kraken's yellow stripes; it was comforting compared to the cacophony of senses.

Like the FCM *Quantor*, it took a while to walk to their destination. She was thankful as Kraken lead her down side tunnels toward quieter areas. The narrower corridors were claustrophobic and comforting, just like the prison tunnels she had grown accustomed too. Despite the more comfortable areas, she kept her hand rested against Kraken's side, right above his shoulder.

At one junction, she peered over her shoulder to look at the others, but somewhere during their walk, Hissa and Gornak had gone their separate ways. She was alone with Kraken. She looked back and caught him looking at her.

She ducked her head and blushed. "Kraken?"

"Yes, Eliza?"

"What am I to you?"

He tilted his head toward her. She peeked up to see the bright blue eye staring directly at her. "Many things."

She rolled her eyes and smiled sheepishly. "I was hoping you would be a little clearer... over here on this ship."

"You think I was waiting to come here to play?"

A nod and she sighed. "Every time I look at you, I think you are playing more games than I can wrap my head around."

"Yes."

Eliza wasn't surprised. "I feel like a pawn."

Kraken tilted his head again. "Everyone start a pawn. The only question is when they decide they want to be more."

"W-Was that my move? On the hanger?"

He chuckled. "It could have been."

"But, I couldn't do anything." She clutched his side, trying to think of what she did wrong.

"Really."

"What was I suppose to do?"

He stopped at a side tunnel. His tail curled around to pull her close. "When you are ready, you will find your game."

"I'm not very good."

"I just like having an opponent among the human."

"Ritan? You play with him all the time."

He smiled.

"I-I'm your opponent?"

His tail slid up the back of her thigh before wrapping around her waist. He pulled her close to press his nose against her cheek. "Yes."

She gasped and stared into his eye. She felt a heat bubbling inside her. It was unfocused inside her body, but she could feel him drawing her closer to him. Her breast ground against his side and she felt trapped.

Eliza pressed her other hand against Kraken's neck. She could feel the thud of his heartbeat. It was a slow, steady beat compared to her rapidly pounding heart.

She stared at his red skin for a long moment. "Why me? I'm not a good opponent for you."

"You can be."

"How? What do you see in me?" She gripped him tighter, her fingernails scraping against his pebbled skin.

He turned so his tail and neck encircled her. She shivered at the closeness. "I see curiosity. In all the month I was on your asteroid, I have seen only one person who still had a flame in her eye. You were the only bright thing in a world of dark mind wrapped in dark cloth. I do not care that you are not one of us, I only see the yellow flower among the rotted leaf."

The world spun around her, violent and shaking. She gripped him tightly. "Y-You really do?"

"Yes."

"I-I couldn't imagine you would ever see that."

"Really." He said in his low, rumbling voice.

She shivered and pressed her thighs together. "You really see me that way?"

"Yes, as I did that first time. Bright yellow—" His head came close again, the brush of his breath against her face. He rested his nose against her cheek, his blue eye swimming in her vision as he breathed against her ear. "—haunted eye—" His jaw opened and he slowly drew his bottom teeth along her cheeks.

Eliza moaned at the touch. The sharp points didn't break skin, but the threat and intensity were as overwhelming as the rest of the ship.

"—and forever bright in my mind."

She gulped, trying to ease the tightness in her throat. "You only saw me once in that... uniform."

"Your prison cloth? Yes. I do not forget."

Eliza inhaled when he identified her color. "How did you know?"

He smiled. "I do not forget anything I see. I was curious of your symbol. Ritan gave us computer access, and it is common knowledge. They do not know how much is reveal by what you teach child. He is not an opponent, he has no curiosity. You..." He thumped her with his tail. "Can be a glorious opponent. One day."

Tears blurred her vision. She sniffed and went to wipe her face off, but Kraken stopped her. Moving his head over, he licked her face. His dry tongue rasped as he trailed along her eyes and over her nose. When he pulled back, the tears were gone.

"Come," he said in a low growl. "You will like my quarter."

Eliza smiled and did a double-take. "Your quarters? Am I staying there?"

He nodded and uncurled from around her. Walking slowly, he headed down a corridor painted red with yellow stripes. "Yes, I think you enjoy sharing my space. It will keep you safe and..." He looked at her, his eyes almost glowing in the dimly light tunnel. "Maybe you can be curious about thing yourself."

She felt her heart thumping as she followed after him.

14 Her Move

As Eliza rolled over, she sank into the thick pillows that cradled her body. Her sleeping outfit caught on the fabric and her weight drew the collar against her throat. The pressure cut off her breath, and she panicked. With a gasp, she pried herself up to free her clothes before dropping back down.

As her mind adjusted to the utterly alien bed, she smiled. The raptors slept on dozens of cushions instead of underneath blankets. Each meter-square pillow felt like a cloud underneath her body, though she was sprawled out more than cuddled. She knew her ass was hooked on the ridge of one cushion and thrust into the air. Her head and hands were below, splayed out in the gaps between the silky fabric.

She felt exposed, but it didn't bring the customary fear. She felt different than before, a strange sense of happiness mixed in with anticipation. Kraken's words echoed across her mind, the strange rumbling cadence mixing in with the ideas he implanted in her head. He wanted her, that part she was sure, but she wasn't sure if it was someone to spar with or have battles of twisting words or... something else.

Eliza moaned and stretched out against the pillows. It was easy to arch her breasts and stick her ass higher in the air. The tension of her sleep outfit tugged against her buttocks and nestled in the crack between her legs. Normally, she wouldn't feel the pressure at all, but with her unconventional position, it ground against the very sex she was to ignore.

She couldn't ignore it now. With another moan, she rocked her hips to one side and the other. The fabric followed her movements, tugging against her breasts and hips as strained to shield her body from her own senses. A fold caught against her clitoris and she moaned louder.

Reflexively, she bit down on the pillow to muffle herself. Kraken's room was a large open area shaped like a cave. His home was a brilliant explosion of flowers, cushions, and rippling fabric. The three-point cavern had sleeping and resting areas at one point, a set of pools in another, with the third dedicated to entertainment. It was also huge, large enough to run and jump for hours without getting bored.

A prick of concern raised the hairs on the back of her hair. Taking a deep breath, she braced herself on the pillows and forced her head out of the sea of cushions. She had to blink to focus on the flowers growing along the edge of the nest that he gave her. In the distance, the sound of rushing water was a counterpoint to a low rumble.

She knew that rumble. With a smile, she looked over one shoulder and then the other. When she saw Kraken stretched out of his own nest, his head resting on the pathway between their two places, she wasn't surprised. "Good morning."

"You look both comfortable and uncomfortable." His voice carried the deep purr that rumbled in his chest.

She looked up at her ass, seeing how he was staring at the cleft of her sex and her upturned buttocks. She inhaled as the heat continued to fill her, tingling along her neglected sex. "No, I think I'm very comfortable."

"Ah, then I must be the uncomfortable one."

She cocked her head and gave a curious smile. "Why?"

Kraken stood up. The cushions rolled off his body as he shook himself and stepped out. Her eyes drifted down his red body until she saw the source of his discomfort. The thick rod of his dick was obvious against his belly. At the sight of it, she clenched her own muscles and felt a strange ache throb.

His body shook the ground as he thudded toward the bathroom area, one of the few side caves to his cavern. Eliza watched as he did, wondering about the process but also struggling against the heat that bubbled inside her.

She slid her hand down the thick fabric of her sleep uniform. She found the bunched fabric of her sex and stroked it, but the material prevented her from feeling anything but pressure. She blushed as she tugged at the fastener, working it open so she could slide her hand down her stomach and between the cushion and her own sex.

Less than two years ago, she was doing the same thing in her ship, but now there was no sense of hurry or concern. There were no recordings or sensors, no threat of the colonel or prison. She closed her eyes as her finger found her damp slit. With a moan, she worked her fingers between the folds and found her clitoris. Stroking slowly, she lost herself in a few stolen seconds of pleasure.

When she heard Kraken's heavy footsteps, she yanked her hand back. Blushing with embarrassment, she fumbled with the fastener.

He crouched down next to her nest and chuckled. "Why do you hide that?"

"W-What?" She looked up at him. He was huge as he loomed over her. Slowly, her eyes trailed down his body to his groin, but the rod had faded. She felt disappointed and brought her eyes back up to the eye he aimed toward her.

"Your pleasuring. There is nothing here to stop you."

"I-I thought that—"

"I would not want to watch?"

At the sudden rush of heat and tingling pleasure, she ground her thighs together.

Kraken leaned over and sniffed. His nose hovered centimeters above her pussy, and she tensed with anticipation. "You smell good."

Bashfully, she spread her legs again. Her position, ass upturned, suddenly took on a new meaning when she realized how easy it was for him to bring his nose to her wet folds.

He purred. "Finish up, if you wish, and join me? I miss a proper bath on your ship." He straightened and thudded away.

She stared at him with shock for a moment. He wanted to watch, she thought, but then he just walked away. Confused, she reached down to masturbate, but then stopped. She wondered if there was a hidden mean in Kraken's words.

Eliza knew he was toying with her, but she still didn't know what he wanted.

Frustrated, she crawled out of the nest with less grace than she hoped. She reached the edge with a stumble and almost fell into Kraken's nest. Blushing, she headed straight for the toilet area. The night before, it took her a while to figure out how to use the water jets to clean, but she quickly fell in love the raptor's bathing area. They used real water to clean and blasts of heated air to dry. Everything was perfumed and soft and sensual.

She finished, washed up, and headed toward the bathing outfit. Her sleeping outfit hung on her body, the sturdy weight tugging down as the hem caught on the flowers or rough rocks underneath her feet. Her bare feet padded across the wide, flat rocks that lead around the cavern.

Her footsteps slowed, and she breathed in the smells of flowers, perfume, and crystalline water. She couldn't find the source, but it didn't matter. The citrus scents blended with muskier smells. With a soft giggle, she twirled around and ran her fingers through the delicate petals on both sides of the trails.

She reached the first pool and peered over a ridge of rocks. It was the cooler of the pools, but Kraken wasn't in the water.

She drew back and started along a trail leading to the higher pools. She pass through steaming waterfalls and trailed her hand through them. The water, almost searing hot, splattered against her hand and soaked the sleeve of her uniform. She giggled and stuck her hand back in, enjoying how the liquid split around her fingers.

A blast of searing liquid poured down on her. She sputtered as she stared up, trying to blink past the perfumed water. It soaked into her sleeping outfit, and it dripped down her skin.

"Hey!" she yelled.

Kraken barked in laughter. She heard the slap against the surface right before another wave of water came over the edge of the waterfall. She stumbled back and lost her balance. She let out a shriek as she landed on a soft, plant-covered rock and rolled back. With an ungraceful thump, she rolled backwards until she planted her hands and knees in a patch of moist dirt and flowers.

Kraken barked again.

She looked up and saw him peering over the edge.

His red head bobbed up and down. "A good position for you."

Confused, she looked back and realized her soaked sleeping outfit clung to her body, highlighting her ass and clinging to her sides. She blushed hotly and scrambled to her feet.

Kraken lowered his head out of sight. "Come, clean yourself up here."

Her cheeks burning, Eliza followed the stone path up to the highest pool. As she came around the curve, she saw a large pool of steaming water. Wide-leaf flowers floated along the surface and white petals bobbed in the ripples.

It took her a moment to see Kraken. Only his head was visible above the water, and his blue eyes were half-submerged. She spotted the tip of his tail, curled back and rising above the water like a scorpion's tail.

She stopped. "Um, hi."

Kraken lifted his head. Water poured down over his skin, tracing the pebbled surface before splashing to the pool. He tilted his head to peer at her with one eye. "Join me."

Looking down at the pool, she grew nervous. There were no baths on the asteroid, it would be too opulent.

He lifted higher, his long neck curling. "Aren't you curious?"

She flushed and nodded.

"Then join me. You will enjoy it."

"Don't I need... an outfit?" She held her soaked sleeping outfit.

Kraken chuckled and lowered his head back to the water.

She felt her nipples grow hard as she looked at him. When his eyes didn't shift from her body, she knew the answer. She tugged on the fastener and tried not to think about her rapid breathing. The warm air tickled her damp skin as she pulled it open.

Kraken's tail curled up higher.

Her body tingled as she slipped it off her shoulder. The soggy fabric clung to her breasts until she dragged it over. As her nipples came free, her small mounds jiggled briefly. She stared at Kraken while pushing her clothes down over her hips and to her knees.

She was naked, but the moist air felt good against her skin. She straightened slowly, fighting the urge to cover her breasts and pubic area. Compared to the time in the bathroom, she felt more at ease with Kraken watching with his unblinking blue eyes. But, the intensity remained and she enjoyed the tingling anticipation that tickled her thighs and pussy.

With a grin, she arched her back and thrust her breasts up. "Do you like?"

He bobbed his head, the water rippling over his top before he surfaced again.

Eliza inched forward to the water's surface. Taking a deep breath, she dipped her toe into it. At the heat, she gasped. "It's hot."

He smiled, the teeth rising above the surface.

She took a deep breath and sank into the water. Every centimeter of hot liquid sent pulses of pleasure through her body. She moaned louder and continued to lower her body. She cringed when the water lapped at her pussy, but then slumped down after the initial sting faded into a hot waves of enjoyment.

Kraken barked into the water, the muted noise bubbling around him. He was laughing at her.

Eliza shot a glare at him. "It's my first time!"

"Yes, and you were exquisite."

Nervously, she smiled. "You were curious how I would look?"

"Are you surprised?"

"No, not anymore." Eliza felt around the bottom of the pond with her hands. The edges were soft and spongy but also smooth. She slipped to the side until she found a spot that cupped her buttocks. The water lapped right underneath her breasts. The realization that Kraken stared at her nipples added to the heat seeping into her body.

She glanced down at her breasts. She could see her legs rippling underneath the water. With a grin, she looked up. "Anything you're still curious about?"

"Yes. Of many thing."

"What?"

He grinned, his teeth visible even through the water. "Are you offering?"

She blushed and looked down at the water. "I like showing you things. It makes me... feel good."

Kraken's tail curled higher. "I can smell."

With a smile, she peeked up through the steam. "So?"

His tail swirled through the water. The passage left ripples across the steaming liquid. He lifted his head and shook the water off. "I did not know it was my turn."

Eliza's smile froze on her face. "It's my turn?"

"If you want."

Eliza shifted on her seat and swirled the water around her breasts and arms. She stared at the ripples, trying to think of what she could ask of the enigmatic raptor. An image rose up in her mind, of him crawling of his nest with the hard rod bulging at his crotch. She blushed and tore her thoughts away. She couldn't ask to see that.

Kraken swirled his tail through the water.

"I-I don't know how to take a move."

"Yes, you do."

She gulped. "I'm scared."

"Good."

"Why?"

"Because it feel better when you learn that it does not hurt to ask."

She pressed her hands against her thighs. A few days ago, she wouldn't have considered touching herself again. Now, if she spread her legs, she knew that Kraken would watch, and she would happily come for him. If she masturbated, he would watch and his attention would bring a knife edge of pleasure. She smiled to herself, listening her breath growing deeper and faster.

Slowly, she inched her knees apart.

Ripples of water swirled over her breasts. She looked up to see Kraken had lowered himself back into the water, but he covered half the distance between them. She could feel the eddies underneath the surface from his movement, like tiny, silken caresses. His body was a crimson blob underneath the steaming ripples.

Her deep breaths shook the surface. She watched as her breasts rose and fell, her skin glistening with water that was too hedonistic for her life before Kraken.

Slowly, she forced herself to lift her gaze to him. Her heart pounded as she struggled with the words. She knew what she wanted. She wanted to feel his cock in her hands, to touch the forbidden part of his body. But, humiliation and embarrassment froze the words.

Kraken said nothing.

Eliza cleared her throat. "C-Could I see your teeth?"

Even as she said it, she felt fear rising inside her. She just asked to see the maw of a creature that could rip out her throat. It was exactly what Ritan hoped for, a bloody death. A whimper threatened to rise in her throat but she fought it down, struggling to maintain her composure in front of the alien.

"Of course." He stepped closer. Waves of water washed over her as he brought his nose to her cheek.

She smiled at the now familiar caress. Closing her eyes, she rested her head against the side of his muzzle. She smiled and tried to calm herself.

He lifted his head, and she opened her eyes just as he opened his mouth. The moist heat washed over her face. She gulped as she peered inside, staring at a jaw larger than her head. Kraken had dozens of teeth, all of them sharp and faintly stained by the endless bloody deaths of his meals.

Fear clutched her stomach, twisting it, but so did a pulsating heat.

Eliza gulped and reached out with one hand. Water dripped off her hand as she poked one of the sharper teeth. It pricked her finger. At the sharp pain, her inner muscles clenched in sympathy. "T-These are very... sharp."

He lowered his head with a gasp. The pebbled surface of his chin bumped against her chest before sliding down.

She gasped, her body growing taut as she stared into his blue eye.

Kraken drew his head down, his mouth opening. She felt the smooth points of his teeth press against her breast, indenting the small mounds. The tips branded her skin.

As he approached her nipple, her breathing grew faster and deeper. She whimpered, soft cries, as she tightened her body with anticipation. She grabbed her thighs, digging into her body as she trembled.

He opened his mouth further until the crinkled aerola of her breast scraped against his teeth. Continuing further, he slid the tips down until he caught her nipples.

She whimpered, the heat searing her insides. She could smell her body even through the water, a musky tang that added to the intensity of his movements.

Kraken froze right as her nipples were about to slip off his teeth. The pricks of pain also brought sparks of pleasure.

Eliza held her breath, terrified of impaling her nipples on his teeth but also desperately wanting more. Her lungs quickly burned but she couldn't stir her eyes away from his azure gaze or her body from the sharp points that pinned her in place.

The water splashed around them as Kraken adjusted his position. The massive bulk slipped against her knees. He was heavy and powerful, an irresistible force that was more of a threat than action. It would take little effort to force her legs apart, but he didn't.

His purr rose up from his chest. The vibrations shook through his teeth, resonating through her nipples. She clenched herself, her hands slipped along her water-slicked thighs to clamp against her sex. Even through the water, she could feel the heat radiating from her body.

Kraken closed his mouth. It took her a moment to realize he was biting down on her nipples until she felt the pricks of his upper teeth pressing down.

She gasped and jerked. Her caught nipples stopped her as his jaw tightened. She shuddered and clutched herself tighter, her fingers plunging into her slick pussy without even a hint of friction.

He held himself still, six hundred kilograms of alien poised to tear her breasts off, and his teeth didn't even move a millimeter.

Trembling, she felt caught. The helplessness ignited a sharp pain inside her, connecting her tortured nipples with her clitoris. She let out a whimper as she plunged her fingers into her sex and rubbed along her folds. Each twist brought her senses into a fiery line. She ground harder and faster, tugging on her clitoris until she writhed in her sharp bondage.

His tail bumped against her hip as he drew it around her. She arched her back to give him room around her body and trembled as he drew her close, pinning her body against his rippled chest. It also kept her helplessly tight to the teeth that threatened to pierce her nipples.

Eliza fingered herself faster. Every movement of her hands sent ripples of movement through the water and her body. She cried out louder as her nipples radiated agony and ecstasy. She tugged and panted and whimpered. Her wrists drove deep into her cunt, two fingers of each hand pumping between her spread thighs.

Her orgasm exploded inside her. She pulled back and screamed. The sharp pain from her nipples only added to the white-hot intensity that ripped through her body, sending every muscle into a spasm. Her thighs clamped down, only to be stopped by Kraken's broad chest.

Unable to close her thighs, her helplessness pushed her further into an orgasm that blurred the world until there was nothing but white and pleasure.

She slumped back, cringing at the pain, but Kraken released her aching nipples before the pain grew too sharp. She thumped against the side of the pond and slid down. Her weight pushed her knees apart until she straddled Kraken's chest and the water lapped at her neck.

With a giggle, she looked up at him. "That was... that was..."

"A good move," he purred. With a twist of his body, he withdrew and sank down at the same time, never letting up the pressure between her legs, but lowering himself until his crimson head bobbed at the same level as her in the water.

Eliza glanced at her nipples. They were red and angry, with a single drop of blood clinging to her left tip. She let out a nervous giggle. "Was I close?"

Kraken bobbed his head. She could feel his throat sliding against her thighs and a shiver of pleasure flared the dying embers of her pleasure.

When he didn't answer, she reached out and held his head. "Did you think about biting me?"

"Of course."

The fear and anticipation bubbled bright. "Did you think about eating me?"

He didn't move. "Of course."

A wave of pleasure exploded inside her.

"I wouldn't, but I am curious."

Without thinking, she leaned forward and kissed him right between the eyes.

Dressing Down

Eliza sat in the middle of her nest, surrounded by pillows. She still vibrated from her orgasm. The low simmering heat had spread out to every part of her body, and she felt tiny sparks of pleasure whenever her thoughts drifted back to the events only an hour before. She rubbed her sore nipples, just to enjoy the ache.

In front of her, jammed into a space between cushions, were her clothes. The shipping crate was marked with her space fighter insignia, but someone had plastered prison paperwork over that before scraping it off. She saw her two lives on top of each other, both of which she dreaded her inevitable return.

"Looking for something?" Kraken peered over the edge of her nest, his blue eyes glistening.

She smiled at him. "Trying to find something to wear when we go out."

"Go as you are."

She was still naked from the bath, her pale skin red from the heat of the water. She focused on her nipples, still hard. The droplet of blood hovered in her memory long after the wound closed and her orgasm faded into the tremors that fluttered in her stomach and along her thighs. She closed her eyes and shivered with the ghost of a memory ripples through her veins.

With a sheepish smile, she shook her head. "I can't go naked in public."

"Why not? Almost every creature on this ship is naked."

"Yeah, but you... don't have..." She struggled with the words. Finally, she sighed. "You don't have these," she cupped her breasts, "or hair." She gestured down at the damp fuzz that clung to her pubic mound.

"True, that is distracting."

"Distracting?" She looked at him with confusion. "How?"

Kraken stretched further into her nest. "Because I am curious how it taste."

A wave of heat surged through her body. She clutched the sides of her crate as she stared at him in shock. "W-What?"

He smiled with bared teeth. "You heard me."

Her mouth opened as she stared at him. She knew what he was talking about, but the idea of his mouth against her pussy sent ripples of fear and lust burning through her body. "I-I..."

"Never thought about my tongue against your body?"

Her cheeks burned as she thought about his tongue rasping against her skin. The idea of the bumps on her nipples, the thickness between her legs, and even his tail wrapped around her sent pulses of pleasure rolling through her body. Her mind struggled with such an alien thought, but her body burned with the sudden need to feel it.

She clenched the box tighter and panted.

Kraken barked out a laugh. "You are now."

Eliza clenched her thighs against the box and gripped the side. "That was mean."

"Really."

She peeked at him and smiled. "Was that your move?"

"Yes." His tail curled up and curled into a question mark. He rested his head on the side of the nest and peered at her. "You look lost."

Eliza glanced back to her box. "I... I don't know what to wear anymore. I... I..." She couldn't explain how the uniform felt wrong at the moment.

"How about dress?"

"D-Dress? What's a dress?"

"Fabric draped over your body and pulled around your waist. It was an archaic outfit from your species past. Quite popular compared to the thick uniform you wear now."

She stared at him for a moment. "How do you know that?"

"What do you think I'm doing in the month I was there? Learning. Learning from your history, political systems, and everything else I can. That way, when we..." He lifted his head. "I am always curious."

With a smile, Eliza made a show of pulling out her uniforms. "I don't see a dress in here." She dropped the thick fabric of her prison outfit. The yellow fabric thumped against her thigh. "Not that I would know what a dress looks like."

Kraken lifted his head and tilted his head so one eye focused on her.

Eliza felt a shiver of something. "What?"

He sighed and lowered his head. "Billie is late."

"Billie? The little one in the ship?"

"Yes, the pilot. You like her?"

She nodded sharply.

"She offered her family to make something. I thought a dress would be nice. But, she was suppose to—"

"Krak!" Billie's high-pitched voice drifted from the entrance.

Eliza jumped at the voice. She stumbled to her feet and peered over the cushions at the entrance.

A swarm of bright blue rolled over the paths in a storm of screeches, jumping, and claws. There were hundreds of tiny raptors, all of them Billie's size. Tiny heads and tails rippled in a wave of blue speckled with yellow.

Eliza felt a smile crossing her face as the carpet of raptors rolled into her nest. She saw some of the smaller ones falling into the cracks of the cushions. More of them jumped on top, clawing and biting and growling in high-pitched voices. They were also talking and snapping, but Eliza couldn't understand what they were saying.

Billie crawled up on top. "Hi, hi, hi, Eliza!"

"Eliza!" screamed the horde of raptors, the only coherent word in the din.

Kraken stood up, his feet thumping on the ground.

The swarms peeled away from the ground, and his claws struck the ground instead of the wiggling carpet of blue and claws.

He let out a sharp roar.

Eliza jumped as did the others. She sat down, her eyes wide as she stared at him.

Peering around, Kraken focused on Billie. He snarled something in the guttural language of the raptors.

Billie bobbed her head and gave a tiny yip.

The swarm of raptors boiled as something fluttered underneath them. It was bright and yellow, but it wasn't alive. It was fabric, and she realized it was the dress that Kraken mentioned.

Curious, Eliza crouched down as the tiny raptors brought it to her. She smiled and picked it up. It was thin and light, nothing compared to heavy material and armored fabrics that she grew up in. She straightened and let it drape over her hand.

It was a brilliant yellow with stripes of red along the sides.

Kraken's head rested on her shoulder, peering at her and the dress at the same time. "Do you like?"

"It's... it's..." She struggled with her words. A tear ran down her cheek. "It's beautiful."

"Yep!" yipped Billie. "My child and I all made it last night!"

Eliza looked at the hundreds of blue raptors wrestling and jumping on the cushions. "Which one?"

Billie cocked her head, her yellow eye focused on him. "My child."

Realization dawned. Eliza looked at them. "All of them?"

"Yep!" bounced Billie. "We all decided to like you."

The swarm cheered with sharp yips and barks.

Billie gestured with her tiny claws. "Come on, put it on."

Her babies, all the hundreds of tiny raptors, repeated her phrase.

Eliza laughed and tried to figure out how to put it on. There were too many holes for her, but she eventually realized which one was the neck hole and where the sleeves were. Gulping, she stood naked among the raptors and slipped it over her head.

The fabric slid down her body, as smooth as water. It was hot from the bodies of the little raptors. The hem and texture caressed every inch of her body. It clung to her nipples and hips and shoulders. Her knees buckled from ecstasy and she dropped. Her shins hit the cushions as the swarm of raptors peeled away.

Billie giggled.

Eliza panted as she trembled, her body shuddered as if she just had an orgasm. She looked up at the hundreds of tiny raptors staring at her. Above them, looming with his crimson body and yellow stripes, was Kraken. Her eyes met his and she smiled.

And then the dress slipped off her shoulder. The collar dragged along her breast before puddling at her knees.

"Oops," said Billie.

Kraken let out a bark of amusement.

"Oh well," Billie said with her tail down. "We will do better next time."

"No," gasped Eliza. She stood up and gathered her dress and pulled it back up over her head. She twisted the fabric for a moment, then moved her head to one of the arm holes. Pulling it down, she used the collar for her left arm and ignored the third hole that left part of her hip exposed.

She struggled for a hole for her right arm before Billie helpfully tore an opening.

Twisting the fabric in place, Eliza looked up at the gathered raptors. "How does it look?"

A trill rippled through the raptors.

Kraken bobbed his head and barked. His tail quivered as it curled up behind him.

16

Overwhelming

Six hours later, Eliza stood next to Kraken and struggled to keep a smile on her lips. A quadruped lizard spoke gutturally at her, but she didn't understand a single word. The lizard's pattern was large blotches of green with a lighter green line raggedly tracing each shape.

The creature bobbed its head and stopped talking.

"Um," Eliza said, "thank you?"

Billie barked from her position across Eliza's shoulders. "Good guess, she was saying she loves your smell."

"I heard the word for beautiful but which one was smell?"

The tiny blue raptor spoke, and Eliza tried to repeat it. Eliza's throat hurt from her efforts to learn the language, which only added to her pulsating headache and the exhaustion plucking at her nerves. After the third attempt, Eliza gave up and bowed her head.

Kraken's paws thudded as he approached. "Very good. Your accent is improving. And she's right, you do smell nice."

Eliza smiled and twisted her hips. Her dress fluttered around her waist, and the silky fabric caressed her thighs. The warm air brushed against her skin, tickling her pubic hairs and reminding her that only a thin material covered her body.

The only weight came from her energy pistol strapped around her hip. Both Kraken and Billie insisted she wear it when she was out of the cavern.

A blush grew on her cheeks as she fluttered her dress again, enjoying the sensation.

She noticed Kraken's tail curling up. Feeling playful, she grabbed the fabric and tugged it up as she tilted her ass toward him. The caress ran up the curve of her buttocks, and the breeze tickled her between her legs.

The tail curled up faster. Then, Kraken grunted and turned away.

In her ear, Billie yipped and curled tighter. "Now," whispered the tiny raptor, "you smell even nicer."

Eliza's cheeks burned.

"And," continued Billie, "he smell good too."

Leaning over, Eliza whispered back, "You know I can't smell anything, right?"

Billie nipped her own tail. "I figured. Would it be better if I said you are a nice color?"

"Yeah, a little."

"I like the yellow. It match my eye."

Eliza glanced at Kraken who spoke with a pair of biped raptors with longer arms and broad heads. His crimson body glistened with the water from a recent dip in one of the many communal pools. She watched the yellow stripes along his back and how they moved with his strips. "They almost match his stripes."

"Oh, you do not want that." Billie's claws caressed Eliza's neck.

"Why?"

"Colors run in family. Same color and pattern, probably related. And given how Kraken is smelling, that would be like lusting after his own daughter."

Eliza inhaled sharply, and she felt a prickle of excitement. "He's smells like that?"

"Really?" Billie said. "You could not figure that out already? He find you attractive, pretty, sexy. A potential mate."

"I may have guessed." Eliza looked at Kraken, enjoying the play of his muscles underneath his pebbled skin. "Maybe hoped."

"And you, smell like you want to mate him too." Billie yipped with amusement.

Eliza smiled broadly. "Really."

It wasn't a question.

17 Curiosity

She never thought a sixteen hour day could be so exhausting when all she did was walk the length of the nest ship. But, between the meeting of new creatures, language lessons from Billie and her swarm of babies, and the occasionally stolen looks to Kraken, she felt as if her veins had been filled with hot lead. She staggered down the stone path from the upper soaking pond. Steam rose off her naked body and splashes of water marked her passing.

Before her, she saw Kraken's paws marking the path. Water and claw prints wound back to the sleeping nests. She reached the point she could see the nests clearly and saw him curling up in his own bowl of cushions, his crimson body forming a circle with his tail resting against his tail.

Eliza stopped and watched the raptor as he settled. She felt hot when she watched him. It was more than the sexual curiosity she had for him, but also the mental. He never said she was flawed or broken. There wasn't even a hint that he thought anything less than her as someone fascinating and, she hoped, intelligent.

It felt good, his attention. She smiled and tapped her foot on the ground to shake water off her toes. She only hoped he wouldn't tire of her or find her tedious.

Stirring herself from her thoughts, she continued down the path. Her bare feet slapped against the textured rocks, and the sound echoed against the cavern walls. She skipped a step and jumped off the trail. The flowers caressed her thighs as she cut off a few meters and then hopped down to the level with the nests.

Kraken's tail had curled up as she approached. She stared at it for a moment and grinned. It seemed to curl when he was excited.

No, she grinned, it curled when he got sexually excited. He quivered when he was simply having fun.

She stopped in the space between the two nests. "Enjoying the view?"

He twisted his body, the six meters rotating until his pale red belly was visible in the dim light. One azure eye peered at her. "Always."

Eliza looked down at her naked breasts and hips. She could see the curls of her pubic hair along her sex. "Anything else you want to see?"

Kraken smiled, his teeth bright in the dim light.

She crouched next to him, fully aware she could feel her labia splitting from her position and exposing her sex to him. "Thank you."

"For what?" His head tilted slightly to watch her body before he drew his attention back up. He sniffed, and she felt a thrill knowing he was smelling her.

She reached out and stroked her hand along his chin. "For making me feel good. No one has ever done that before."

"Really."

With a giggle, she turned and dropped to her knees. She crawled into her own nest and dug into the cushions. Finding a comfortable spot, she curled and brought her knees up to her chest. Seeing that Kraken had assumed the same position, she grinned and tried to twist her body in a similar posture. She buried her face into the cushion cracks, though she didn't have his flexibility so her ass rose up.

Kraken chuckled, a deep rumbling noise, and she heard him settle back down.

She grinned and freed her face. "Were you just looking at me?"
"Of course."

Her breathing came faster. "Did you watch me all day?"
"Yes."

"Is that why your tail curls up when I'm not looking?"
Silence.

She smiled to herself. "That means you want me, doesn't it?"
"Yes." A purr rumbled through the air. "I do."

Twisting herself on her back, she pressed one hand against her sex. She could feel the heat and hairs tickling her palm. Slowly, she drew her finger up the folds that were just beginning to tingle with excitement. She could imagine his tail curling up and the hard rod of his cock growing. At the thoughts, she pressed her finger harder and parted her labia. Slowly, she trailed her fingers up until she found her clitoris. She stroked herself with slow movements. "What do you want me to do?"

A faint chuckle. "Answer a question."

Eliza stared up at the ceiling, her fingers still moving. "A question?"

"Yes." When she encouraged him, he continued. "This morning, you had a choice and you wanted to see my teeth."

The memories welled up and her pussy grew slick and hot almost instantly. She moaned and forced two fingers into her pussy, pumping with short, deep strokes.

"Why?"

Eliza stopped at the sound of his voice. She could hear the curiosity in his voice, confusion resonating in the deep rumble. She thought back to the morning and her struggle. Twisting, she recalled the humiliation and fear of being too curious. Taking a deep breath, she said, "I was curious."

"About what?"

"I... I was curious about your..." She blushed even though he couldn't see her. Her heart pounded as she felt exposed in the dim light and buried in cushions. "I wanted to see your penis."

Nothing.

Silence stretched out for long moments, and she was terrified she said the wrong thing.

And then he chuckled. "Really."

Hand still planted on her sex, she giggled. "You knew?"

"I guessed, but I do not know why you avoided asking."

"I was scared."

"I won't bite."

She giggled and clutched her breast with her other hand. "You did bite!"

"Did it feel good?"

"Yes," she moaned.

He said nothing in return.

She closed her eyes and stroked her sex. It was a slow, languished movement that brought little sparks of pleasure running along her nerves. She pictured his sheath swelling with excitement.

A heat tickled her skin and her juices welled up around her digit. She stroked her clitoris with two fingers, moving faster as she tried to imagine what it would look like when it slipped out. Would it be hot? Slick? What would it smell like?

And then she realized he would be more than willing to let her find out.

Her heart thumped harder in her chest. She pulled her hand away and brought her dripping fingers to her mouth. Tasting herself, she stared at the ceiling and screwed up her courage. "Kraken?"

"Yes, Eliza?"

"Can I see it?" She shivered as the last word passed her mouth.

The purring grew louder. "Yes."

She squeezed her thighs together. Trembling, she rolled on her stomach and pushed herself up. Planting her hands and knees, she crawled over the cushions to the edge. Her legs kept slipping into the cracks but she clawed her way to balance on the ridge. "N-Now?"

Kraken was looking at her. He bobbed his head in agreement and then lifted his head. His neck formed a curved that welcomed her to his nest.

Heat blossomed through her body and her skin tingled with anticipation. Panting, she crawled out of her sleeping area and over the warm stone tiles to his. With a trembling hand, she reached out and ran her palm along his pebbled surface.

His solid body shook with the deep purr that rumbled in his chest. She could feel the vibrations through her palm and into her body. His claws were buried in the cracks of the cushions but she knew his teeth were centimeters away.

She shivered at the memory of him biting her. Panting, she hesitated before crawling against his body before slumping down in the ring that his body made. Her back thumped against his tale as she settled down less than an arm's length away from the one thing she wanted to see.

Kraken lowered his head and settled it down, encircling her and watching with one blue eye.

Her throat tightened even as her body tingled with anticipation. She couldn't look down at his belly. Instead, she gave him a pleading look.

"Do not rush, do not do what you do not want to do." His voice shook his nest, the vibrations rolling across her body.

The feeling of being trapped increased, but so did her excitement. She caught whiffs of her excitement rising, the musky and tangy scent that Kraken teased out of her with every move he made. She giggled softly, feeling foolish and excited and terrified.

Kraken made no effort to move or push her forward, and that simple inaction was enough to draw her attention to satisfying her curiosity. Turning her body, she leaned back against his chest. The vibrations shook her entire frame, but it only added to the intensity as she stroked her palm down his soft belly. Unlike the pebbled surface of his head and back, his stomach felt more like the softest leather she had ever touched. It was as sensual as the dress that Billie made her; a surge of heat flared inside her as she traced her fingers down to the bulge already forming between his back legs.

It was hotter than the rest of his body, almost searing despite the skin between her and his penis. The sheath felt soft underneath her touch, but the bone-hard rod inside was more than she expected.

Eliza let out her breath in a gasp of surprise. She brought her other hand around to caress it, exploring his length still buried in his sheath. Her breath came in loud pants as she worked her fingers down, feeling the veins through the soft skin. There were no bulges or bumps, only a thick rod the width of her wrist.

Her pussy clenched. The moisture leaking out tickled her skin. She could feel it gathering against her swollen labia before dribbling out and teasing her before soaking into the cushions.

Around her, Kraken's breathing grew deeper and louder. It pulsed in time with his purrs, a rumbling that prickled her fingers with every wave of rumbling noise.

She worked her way the length. He was about a meter in length with his penis growing thicker with every centimeter toward his tail. By the time she reached the mid-point, she could barely stretch her fingers around the hardness. The heat boiled underneath her, and she knew she would burn herself if his sheath wasn't there to protect her.

Eliza had to pull herself away to reach the base. She shifted so she was kneeling on the cushions, her ass resting on the ridge of his tail. Her nipples and clitoris ached with every roll of his purr. She spread her legs for balance, but also to bring air to her dripping sex.

Curiosity continued to drive her as she continued down. The base of his cock was thicker than she expected, wider than her thigh, and far larger than could ever fit inside her.

She bit her lip as she realized where her thoughts were going. She wanted him inside her, to feel the heat burning her from the inside. She panted louder, the sweat prickling along her skin, as she curled her fingers to where his length anchored to his body. Next to thickest part, she felt his testicles nestled into two soft pouches, protected by the meat of his belly. When she caressed them, they jumped underneath her touch.

"Careful," growled Kraken, "they are sensitive."

With a nod, Eliza drew her fingertips back up his length. "Does it come out?"

"When I'm excited."

She ran her fingers along the entire meter length, feeling it quiver underneath her touch. "It gets hard when you're excited, right?"

"Yes," he rumbled.

"But not as excited as when it comes out."

He chuckled and drew his head closer. At the same time, the tip of his tail curled around her waist, sliding through the sweat that had gathered at the junction of her legs. It was cool compared to his penis. It pushed between her legs and rested against her sex. The contract of his body and hers was ice and fire and she shuddered as tremors of pleasure coursed through her body.

She gulped as the tail wormed against her sex. Despite working around her body, there was no hesitation as he drew a few centimeters of textured length against her clitoris.

"Yes," he answered next to her head. His breath washed over her skin, tickling the sweat along her breasts and sending sparks of pleasure along her nerves.

She moaned and gripped his hardness with both hands. Her right hand slipped along the opening of his sheath, a slit that radiated a wet heat. It was already slick. With a light touch, she drew her fingers back and forth, timed to match the rubbing of his tail against her clitoris. She leaned into his strokes, her hips moving in slow motion as she imagined his hardness poised to enter her.

Eliza had never had sex with a man. Her fingers, yes. Her brush and various tools in her bedroom, but never with a living, breathing male. She never expected it to happen; there was no room for sex on the asteroid. Now, with her hands on a magnificent length, she felt nothing but a desire to fulfill the primal need that clenched her pussy and brought a quickening to her breath.

She dipped her finger in the slit. When she pulled out, a cloudy liquid clung to it. Strands connected his opening to her fingers. She stared at it for a moment, then dipped her finger back into the heated opening.

Kraken's tail dragged up and down her clitoris, working deeper into the folds of her sex. She leaned into each movement, enjoying the texture as it sent sparks flooding through her. Her toes curled, and she sank down, desperate to feel him slid into her.

But he didn't do more than stroke.

"How," she gasped, "could I get it out?"

He chuckled, his body tightening around her. He thrust hard and fast before returning to the slow, teasing movements. "Not tonight."

With a whimper, she looked up. "Why?"

"Neither of us are ready for that move."

Disappointment flooded through her. She clutched his length and teased his opening, not understanding his reluctance. She wanted him. She needed to feel him inside her, filling her to the brim. His length was more than her body could handle, but she also had no doubt that he would be as precise as biting her nipples, exactly what they needed and nothing more.

"Though, if you want to see me orgasm, that is a move we can take."

She panted and stroked his length with her left hand, rubbing her palm along the heated skin from base to tip and back again. "How?"

His entire body shuddered. He panted and drew his head tight against her cheek until they were both staring at his length. "Like that," he whispered in a low rumble. "Just keep stroking."

"How about this?" she whispered back, not wanting to break the mood. She used her right hand to finger his slit, pumping in and out as if it was her pussy. As she pushed past the second knuckle, she felt the tip of his cock. It was a blunted tip and searing hot. Liquid swirled around her fingers, clinging to her skin as she withdrew.

The shudders continued, rippling down the length of his body.

She smiled, feeling giddy and excited. "Just like that, right?"

"Just like that." His tail slipped further past her hip and began to take longer strokes. He drew back and forth against her clitoris and opening, strumming them like a bow of an ancient fiddle.

Her body hummed with his manipulations. She rocked into his movements, enjoying the sound of slurping that echoed in her ears. It matched with the wet slick that bubbled out of his slit and coated her right hand. She added a second finger to his slit, driving in and out with rapidly increasing strokes. Every time she buried herself to her knuckles and struck his cock, the entire length seemed to pulse with heat.

No words were needed as she pumped and fingered him. She rocked her hips in time with her strokes, imagining it was his cock inside her.

Kraken's tail matched her movements, drawing along her clitoris with every stroke. She knew it was dripping with her juices; she could smell it filling the space enclosed by Kraken's body. His own scent mixed in with hers, a sharp musky scent that grew stronger with every surge of his precum oozing between her fingers.

It took her a moment to realize his purring had gotten deeper. She always thought it was a rumble, but now the bass felt like it was beating in her chest and pulsing through her body. It throbbed, rising and lowering in volume in time with her strokes. It was intense sensation, adding to the intensity of her stroking an alien with her bare hands.

"I am..." he said, but she didn't need words to know he was about to come. His cock had grown thicker and hotter, straining against his sheath. His tip swelled and reached for the opening, just peeking out.

Eliza was already lost in an orgasm brought on by his tail. She whimpered through clenched teeth as she strained to bring him to an orgasm. The pleasure ripped through her, sending her entire body into a spasm.

She could barely focus on the hard rod, but her hands worked with the reflexive need they both shared.

Kraken shuddered violently, the movement going from his head to his tail. As it reached her clit, it seemed to sink into her body and shook her from the inside. His breathing turned into a panting growl. She could feel the cushions shift underneath her as he pawed at the softness underneath her body.

Eliza clamped her thighs together, still enjoying the orgasm that ripped through her. She saw stars gathering in her vision and her body strained to lock into a final surrender, but she couldn't release it until he came. She didn't know how much, but she wanted to see Kraken orgasm.

Without warning, Kraken nipped at her shoulder. His sharp teeth scraped against her shoulder, leaving lines of burning pain to mix in with the pleasure already storming through her. At the same time, he drove forward in her hands. His cock head, nestled in the ring of his slit, swelled before shooting out a hard jet of thick semen against her hands. It splashed and flooded through her fingers, squirting everywhere.

The smell, sharp and tangy, filled her lungs as she gasped at the sensation. He came hard again, scoring a line of cum against her palm. It was thick as pudding and clung to her skin. It was also hot, almost boiling, and she felt the pain adding to the scratches along her shoulder and her orgasm that finally created.

With a cry of pleasure, she slumped against his body and stared at the thick cum that pooled in her hand.

Kraken took a deep breath, the movement lifting her body, before he exhaled. "Thank you."

She nodded as the last of the orgasm tremors faded. Her body was slick and hot, tingling with the afterglow. She couldn't take her eyes away from his cum. It felt slick against her hand. "There isn't a lot," she breathed.

"Not unless I get excited."

She looked up. "This isn't excited for you?"

"I am very excited, but I can be more... if the condition right."

"Then, how can I make you more excited?" she asked with a smile. As she stared at him, she brought her hand up to her mouth. The smell of his orgasm flooded her, but she felt a thrill as she drew her tongue through the puddle.

He tasted sharp, but it was the low growl of primal need that shook the air that brought another ripple of an orgasm. Against her thigh, she felt his cock surge again, splattering thick cum against her skin as she lapped at his cum.

"That," he growled, "is a very good start."

Echoes of a Prisoner

Eliza hummed to herself as she strode down the tunnel from Billie's cavern. Her stomach rumbled with contentment from a large dinner, and her head felt just as full from the lessons on the guttural language of the fleet. She knew the names of the creatures she passed, though she still translated them into her own language first: raptor, broton, crawd, and chule.

The raptors were the easiest; they walked on two legs with a long tail and sinewy neck. Almost all were carnivores like Kraken or scavengers like Billie. Though, it surprised her that both Kraken and Billie were races of the same species; they could mate if they wanted.

The brotons were heavy quadrupeds and only ate plants, much like Eliza did on the ship. Their meals were far richer than the raw meats of the raptors. Even after three weeks on the nest ship, she had yet to find an identical meal placed before her. And, of the three types of meals, the salads and plants were far more palatable than the still-living meat for the carnivores.

Crawds were snake-like creatures which spent most of their times in different areas, but she encountered more than a few on her tours with Kraken. They were all pleasant to her, so far, but she felt some deep fear whenever she saw them slithering along the tunnels.

The last were the chules, a catch-all category that included herself. In the centuries of the nest ship jumping from one part of the universe to the other, they had picked up a number of alien species that weren't descended from the lizards or dinosaurs of far-away planets. There were mammals, some of them similar to her own, but also others that had too many limbs or even fewer. She met a furry snake with blunted teeth who spoke in a strange, dual-tone voice.

Eliza had to admit, the last three weeks had been a storm of over-whelming color but also a pleasure of seeing a world that wasn't driven by strict schedules and self-control. She had seen creatures of all kinds fighting, chasing, and fucking in the public areas. There were fights and passion, all of them passing in a wave before fading.

She felt like she had finally found a home.

Her joy faded. The FCM would never let her stay on the ship. Sooner or later, something would happen and Ritan would once again throw her in prison or have her executed. She wished she could stay, but the uncaring asteroid a few gigameters away loomed over her future.

Lost in thought, she continued down the side tunnels toward Kraken's. Her dress fluttered against her hips. She had grown used to not wearing anything underneath it. Her nipples tented the thin fabric, and the moist heat tickled her sex. She loved the sensation; it gave her the illusion of freedom.

The only weight was her pistol. It hung on her left hip and pinned her dress. Every time she left the cavern, she wore it, but there was no reason for Kraken's or Billie's insistence. It felt useless, but she didn't have the courage to leave it behind "accidentally."

Her bare feet slapped against the moist rock as she headed through the tunnel underneath one of the many rivers that coursed through the nest ship. The water-filled tunnels were not only home to some of the unnamed amphibious creatures that resided in the ship, but the tunnels also provided the constant supply of water to fill the endless steaming pools that all the ship occupants enjoyed.

A chitter echoed down the hall.

Eliza slowed for a moment, then continued. There was always some creature walking in the tunnel. She let herself drift to thoughts of teasing Kraken that night. They had joined sleeping nests since that night when they came together. On more than one occasion, they would stroke each other into an orgasm until falling asleep.

Billie knew what they were doing, from the smell, but she only gave sly tips on pleasing a raptor twenty-times her length.

With a smile, Eliza thought about Billie's last suggestion. She never thought about using her mouth against Kraken's slit, but she was willing to do anything to get his rod to slip out. She had already become accustomed to his taste, and the sight of her licking his cum always brought a fresh surge from his cock.

When she heard the scratch of claws in the tunnel, Eliza broke out of her fantasy and her senses came into sharp focus. She expected to be surrounded by the constant flow of creatures, but the tunnel was empty. Lights flickered above her, dimming and brightening with a regularity that felt wrong.

She stopped and peered down the way she came. There was nothing but pipes and conduits on both sides of the tunnels, obscuring the smoothed stone carved out hundreds of years before.

Her skin prickled, and she freed her gun. "Is there someone there?"

A chitter echoed down the hall. She turned to face it, but then stopped when she heard the scratch of claws behind her.

Fear pumped through her veins and she tensed with anticipation.

A small raptor came down the tunnel, its tiny head bobbing as it centered itself in the tunnel. "Pretty meat walking in tunnel alone." The high-pitched voice sent a bolt of fear through Eliza.

The raptor had an emerald green skin with bright yellow eyes. A yellow pattern ran down its belly, from throat to tip of tail. It was unarmed but there was something about the bobbing movement and lowered tail that increased Eliza's growing fear. Raptors raised their tails when they were friendly or excited, not lower it close to the ground.

"Yes, I see it," said another high-pitched voice behind her. "Pretty meat. Stupid meat."

Eliza fought back a scream and spun around. There was four small raptors behind her, about twenty meters away. They shared the same coloration as the first one, a family unit. They were all bobbing as they walked toward her, and their tails dragged against the ground.

Thinking furious, Eliza looked over her shoulder. When she saw a dozen raptors had joined the first one, her heart thumped. She looked up and around, trying to find some way for signaling for help, but there was nothing.

She released the safety on her gun and considered it. The battery on the pistol could handle thirty shots in rapid succession before it needed to recharge. If she slowed her shots, she could double the number of times she fired before burning out the battery.

"Pretty meat," echoed the raptors. There were now dozens of them walking toward her, a carpet of green. They were in no hurry with her trapped between the two swarms. She spotted more of the coming down a tunnel, a seemingly endless stream of tiny raptors.

Eliza's breath came faster. She had never been in danger before. She always wondered how she would respond in situations like this, but to her surprise, panic didn't drown out her thoughts. Instead, she played through Duncan's training lessons that he used to whisper across their bunks growing up.

The first thing she needed to do was call for help. If she couldn't, then no one would know that she was in danger. She had nothing but her dress and her gun. There were no call buttons or communicators.

"Trapped meat," said the first raptor. There were hundreds of them now, a carpet of green rippling at her from both directions.

Eliza spotted emergency sensors along the ceiling. They were to detect a leak from the river above her. With the moisture, she guessed that more than one needed to active to set off the warnings by whoever was monitoring the system. Each sensor was less than a centimeter in size, but a dim light marked their presence.

Gulping, she glanced around. She didn't have enough shots for the rapidly approaching raptors.

She took a deep breath and another, her body trembling with anticipation.

A wave of ripples ran along the raptors. They were less than three meters away.

Fear washed through her and then faded, leaving an empty sensation. It felt like the fighter pilot drills when she learned how to shoot targets in space with the fighter. She only had a few seconds to do something before the raptors attacked her.

Snapping her arm up, she shot the nearest sensor. The pistol flashed and the sensor exploded as a shot of compressed plasma struck it. She spun on her bare feet and shot another sensor.

As the pistol flashed, the raptors pulled back and growled. The high-pitched echo was terrifying when it came from a hundred throats.

Eliza struggled with her fear, spun around, and aimed for the next sensor. She skipped the one next to the smoking one and exploded the one beyond it. She hoped skipping sensors would indicate something other than a leak was happening.

Stepping into the middle of the tunnel, she turned and fired again, skipping them. Her jaw ached as she struggled to hold her breath to avoid spoiling aim.

She was spinning when the first of the raptors jumped for her. With a twist of her wrist, she aimed and blew the raptor in mid-shot. A split-second later, a second blast of plasma took out the sensor.

Turning back, she saw more of them jumping for her. She fired as fast as she could, picking three of them out of the air before shooting at the sensor. She thought she missed and fired again.

She spun back just as the first one hit her. Tiny claws dug into her arm. She snapped her hand back, tossing it away and aimed for the sensor.

One of the raptors jumped on her gun, spoiling her aim. The plasma burst wildly against the stone wall. It did nothing but scorch the stone.

Crying out, Eliza fired into the raptors jumping for her. She picked them out of the air as the weight of impact took her from behind and her legs. Heartbeats later, she felt the pierce of teeth digging into her limbs.

Staggering back, she fired. She didn't miss but she could see the pistol's charge rapidly running out. She couldn't slow down to let it recharge, instead she continued to figure until the weapon died in her hand.

Raptors swarmed over her, biting and tearing at her. She couldn't see anything besides the green and yellow. She yanked at the creatures, throwing them off, but they continued to pour over her.

Her back slammed against the side of the tunnel. She felt a pipe dig into her back. She let out a scream, trying to shield her face even as she kicked and lashed out.

The screeches were deafening and the smell of blood and scorched bodies filled the air.

For a moment, Eliza saw Ritan laughing as he read the report. He knew that Kraken would be forced to give the secrets of the jump drive as an apology. Anger surged through her. She couldn't let Ritan win. Grabbing the nearest raptor, Eliza spun around and slammed it against the wall. She felt bones crunching in her hand, and she dropped it to grab another. The second raptor's back snapped over the pipes lining the wall.

Teeth tore at her skin. Tiny bites, but it wouldn't take much to rip her open. She felt claws going for her throat, her breasts, and abdomen.

Desperate inspiration slammed into her. Blindly grabbing the nearest pipe with both hands, she yanked at it. Muscles hardened by months of hard labor screamed out as she planted her foot and pulled with all her might. It refused to move, but she braced both feet against the wall and pulled until muscles tore and her body exploded into pain.

The pipe snapped from the wall, followed by a blast of high-pressure water. She flew back and slammed against the far wall. The impact knocked off most of the raptors attacking her. She sputtered and pried herself from the stream of water, pulling to the side until she freed herself.

Panting, she wiped the water from her face and looked down at the raptors bobbing. With a snarl, she screamed. It was a pathetic sound compared to what Kraken could do, but the raptors took a step back.

Eliza took a step and brought the pipe down on the nearest raptor. It slammed into the ground, crushing the tiny creature into a splatter of blood. Without hesitating, she slammed her pipe down and crushed another. She kicked at the nearest one and charged into the swarm.

If she was going to die, she was going to kill as many of the fuckers as she could.

Her world became nothing but pain and blood. She smashed bodies as fast as she could swing, crushing them against the floor and walls. When a wave of raptors swarmed over her, she fell back into the water to use the pressure to scrape them off. Before her attackers could regain their feet, she stepped back out of the water and resumed smashing.

The ringing of the pipe became a rhythm to her attacks. She felt bites and slashes across her skin. Her blood added to the stench of blood and gore. She couldn't think through the pain, but she could keep pounding. Her muscles knew the actions, months of mining took over when she couldn't see anymore. She pounded anything that moved, anything that came near her.

A tiny raptor bit down on her hand. She grabbed it by the throat and crushed it against the wall. As the blood splattered her face, she felt more of them jumping on her back. She spun and slammed her shoulders into the wall, crushing the raptors against the pipes.

She staggered as more came from them. Drawing back her pipe, she slammed down.

Only to fall as the pipe stopped moving.

Eliza screamed as she staggered to her feet. She clutched at the pipe, trying to free it. She didn't know why it wasn't moving, she couldn't see through the blood, but she couldn't stop. They would get to her.

A roar slammed into her. It wasn't the squeak of a tiny raptor, but the overwhelming power of a full-sized raptor screaming into her face. She felt the breath washing over her and the sense of something looming.

Eliza stopped with a whimper. She cried out, releasing the pipe to shield her face.

"Eliza!" It was Kraken.

Gasping, she pawed at her face, trying to clear her face. "K-Kraken!?"

"Stop!"

She couldn't. Her body hummed with adrenaline. It pounded in her veins, filled her with a sense of danger and anger. She whined and pawed at her face, not feeling anything besides pressure on her face.

Water splashed into her. She gasped and staggered back, slamming into the blood-soaked walls of the tunnel. Gasping, she peered through the water to see Kraken holding the pipe in one claw. The metal was scarred and ragged, the result of hitting stone and bone too many times. Blood poured down the side and puddled underneath his feet.

At their feet was nothing but bodies floating in the blood and water. There were some raptors alive, but most of them were still with crushed bodies and bones sticking out of their green hides. She couldn't count the bodies, there were too many, but there were more dead than dying.

Trembling, she forced her gaze up to Kraken. He was snarling, his tail low to the ground. She whimpered. "I-I'm sorry," she whispered. "I had to save myself."

A pair of raptors and a broton rushed behind Kraken, heading for the water jetting out of the broken pipe. The broton dove into the water and blocked the jet of water with its body. The two raptors joined in to fix the sealed pipe as the water poured off the broton.

Kraken's tail snapped around. He turned to Hissa, who stood nearby with a broad-muzzle energy rifle in her hand. He spoke sharply in a booming growl. Eliza didn't know all the words, but she heard the tone. He was furious.

She whimpered and stepped back. Her injuries were beginning to push past the adrenaline and she felt the cuts and wounds. Shaking, she looked down. She was covered in bites and cuts. Her blood sheeted down her front, soaking everything. Individually, her cuts were insignificant, but they covered her entire body. She even had claw marks against her inner thighs, and she could feel sharp pains coming from her labia.

With a sob, she sank to the ground.

Kraken's landed next to her. "Eliza!"

She looked up, her body shaking. "I'm sorry."

"No!" he roared.

"I killed... your people."

"No," he snaked his tail around her and pulled her up, dragging her to his body. "You saved yourself. You fought, like you should. You did good."

The world spun around her.

"You did good. You did good," were the last words she heard before darkness swallowed her.

19 Fury

Ritan's mottled face loomed in front of her, filling the video screen. The purple had reached clear down to his neck, and veins bulged out from the tense muscles.

Eliza couldn't help but focus on the bit of spittle clinging to his lip as she waited for the video feed to finish transmitting between the two ships. The two second delay for a single statement was noticeable during her normal reporting, but now that she had reported on her attack, the wait was agonizing.

Her injuries still burned through the painkillers running through her veins. She knew most of the tiny bites and slashes were underneath gauze, but it also meant that most of her body was covered in gray medical fabric. She also had to wear her uniform while making her report. Ritan would have yanked her back in an instant if he knew she wore a dress on the ship. She was careful to keep that out of her report; she wouldn't let him ruin the small measure of happiness she finally found.

On screen, the image flickered and then his voice cut through her thoughts. It wasn't screaming, but fury strained his voice. "Captain Midoze 73, I should have had you executed the day you were born."

She said nothing. Remaining standing was hard enough, but she couldn't respond without jamming herself deeper into the hole.

He stood up and the camera followed. "You killed sixty-seven occupants of that ship!" His voice rose into a bellowing scream. "Sixty-seven! You were assigned there as a liaison to bridge the gap of peace, not initiate a war and put us in a position of weakness."

What wasn't said is that he wanted her to die. He wanted her bloody death to force Kraken to give up more of the fleet secrets. He probably would have had his first orgasm seeing the forensic photographs later.

"Because of your inability to control your genetic flaws, you have forced me to kiss that lizard's ass to save this from being a complete cluster-fuck!"

Eliza blinked with surprise. She had never heard Ritan swear before. She didn't know if that meant his façade had cracked or she had just signed her death warrant.

He sat down heavily. "You have brought this on yourself."

She tensed, waiting for the words.

"I will submit you to the the laws of the raptors. If you survive—" He paused.

Her stomach twisted in her gut, and she fought to remain standing.

"—then you will have a single assignment left for the rest of your... short life. Do you understand?"

She nodded. "Y-Yes, sir."

"You better hope there is mercy among those creatures. There won't be any here. You may have ruined everything, captain. Dismissed."

The screen went dark.

Eliza wanted to drop to her knees and cry. She stood there, staring at the black screen. It didn't turn on again; there was no additional message.

She felt dead inside. She stepped back and winced from the pain of her injuries. Turning around, she walked out of the room they set aside for her reports. It was a short walk back to Kraken's cavern.

Of all the things she fears, Ritan's anger was the least of her worries. She thought about Kraken. She didn't understand his words or his response. He seemed almost... proud that she killed so many raptors.

She padded through the door and looked around. "Kraken?"

"Upper pool!" came his rumbling call.

She trudged up the stairs, head low.

"It did not go well?" Kraken sat in the pool, his entire body submerged up to his head. Water lapped along his bottom jaw and she found herself focusing on the bright blue eye that regarded her.

Eliza shook her head. "I'm being—"

A high-pitched beep cut through the room. Kraken held up his tail and looked at her.

She nodded at the silent question.

With a deft movement, his tail snaked out and wrapped around her waist. Firmly, he pushed her a half meter to the side before unwrapping from her body. Another deft movement pressed a hidden button that Eliza didn't know about.

With a hiss, a large screen project rose out. The top ridge was shaped to match the rocks surrounding the pool. She did a double-take as she looked at it and then back at Kraken.

"While we prefer the appearance of our home, there is an art to blending technology. Now, be silent."

She nodded. He had pushed her out of sight of the camera, but she could see the screen's glow reflecting off the pool.

A brief hiss and the screen changed. She spotted Ritan's reversed face projected against the rippling surface. "Fleet Master Kraken, I'm sorry to use a priority call, but it has come to my attention from Captain Midoze 73's report that I have made a mistake in assigning her to you."

Eliza shivered at the hard words. She started to step back away from the pool.

Kraken bobbed his head, rippling the water and obscuring Ritan's face. His tail slid along the ground until it came up to Eliza's leg.

She stared down at it, confused about his thoughts and actions.

Lifting his head from the water, Kraken growled. "And this would be concerning what, Colonel?"

"She has senselessly murdered sixty-seven of your crew members. I did not know I had a serial murderer among my people, but I swear that I would have had her destroyed years ago if I knew."

"I regret, Rit-tan, that it has come to this. The attack is a serious matter and one that will require some investigating." Kraken's tail snaked up Eliza's body. His facial expressions were serious, and the water barely rippled as he reached for her throat.

Eliza stood there, trembling.

Kraken's tail wormed its way into her collar and then he brought it down, opening the fastener and peeling open her uniform. The textured tip ran along the bandages that covered her body, prickling the skin underneath.

She panted, stunned by his action. As she began to cry out, she clamped her hand over her mouth.

"If there is anything," Ritan continued, "I can do to apologize for this horrid lapse of judgment, I would be—"

Kraken straightened. "There is, Rit-tan."

"A-Anything, Fleet Master Kraken."

"As you know, when your previous liaison were killed on my ship, your superior demanded some form of compensation for their death." As Kraken spoke, he worked Eliza's uniform off her shoulders and tugged it down. The movements were graceful and light, avoiding her injuries as the heavy material slumped against her hips.

She shivered with confused anticipation.

"O-Of course, Fleet Master Kraken." Eliza didn't need to see to know that Ritan's face was beginning to grow purple again.

"I would request an equivalent in exchange."

"Naturally, I would be glad to share information. Do realize that I cannot give anything classified—"

"Like asking for the internal plan of our jump drive?"

Ritan's face paled. "Um, like... that."

Kraken's lips peeled back and Eliza felt fear at the look he gave Ritan. "I do not care about your classification, Rit-tan. In three week time, the fleet will be jumping again and we will never see each other again. I have a list of thing I demand and, unlike your request, they are only common item instead of precious secret."

"T-Thank you, Fleet Master Kraken."

Kraken bowed. As he did, his tail finished removing Eliza's uniform. He brought his tail up her inner thigh, tracing the gray lines of her bandages until he reached her sex.

The attack on Eliza had torn one of her labia, but left her mostly uninjured. She could see feel the burning line of her bisected labia, but it was nothing compared to the confusion and fear she felt.

Suddenly, Kraken's tail withdrew to flip a keyboard over from a rock. He typed rapidly with the tip of his tail, almost as fast as Eliza did on the fateful day in her ship. A moment later, he finished and returned to worm his tail between her legs. He stroked slowly, keeping his member on the less painful side of her sex.

Ritan frowned as he read this. "These are simply manufacturing items: for toys, low-grade robotics, chip assembly plants, and meat growth cubicals. These are..."

"Not secret of your genetic breeding? Or your weapon system?"

"Yes, I mean, no. I'm confused."

Kraken smiled, though Eliza didn't know if it was him playing against Ritan or his tail worming underneath her bandages to find her clitoris. He found it and circled around it, a lazy touch that didn't mar the serious look on his face.

She spread her legs to relieve the pressure. Soft gasps vibrated her palm, but she didn't dare release it.

"You see, Rit-tan, the fleet has no interest in your sterile and bland reproduction. And while your weapon have a faster recharge rate, it requires rare material that you mine from your asteroid. We do not have access to those element, so it would be useless to ask."

"I see." Ritan let out a sigh of relief. "Thank you for being understanding."

"We are but ally for a few short month. Neither of us will meet again once fleet jump, but I see no reason to have a spoiled relationship until then."

Ritan said, "Thank you again. I didn't expect your response or generosity."

Kraken's tail twisted and worked down to Eliza's pussy. She tensed, waiting for the pain, but the drugs in her system pushed back the agony to a discomfort. Her body struggled with the unfamiliar sensations, the pain of her injuries fighting with the rapidly increasing heat and wetness from his deft touch.

"If there is nothing else, I have an investigation to perform."

"Um," Ritan said, "one last question, but it is a personal one."

The tail slipped a millimeter into Eliza's pussy. She clamped her other hand over her mouth and nose to avoid crying out. It was the first time she ever had a living being inside her body, and the pleasure was incredible. She felt swollen and filled as the pebbled surface of his tail teased her sensitive nerves.

"For the crime of murder, what is the punishment?"

Eliza tensed, anger bubbling up inside her.

Kraken cocked his head. "Our sentence for serious crime are common. We strip the murderer naked and then let them go."

"Oh." Ritan sounded disappointed.

"After a few minutes to get ahead, we set the victim's families after them to tear the murderer apart. In the cases of larger family, it can take one or two day of running before the scream start. Then, maybe a day for the scream to stop. It is quite bloody, and we record it to watch later."

As Kraken spoke, Ritan's smile grew wider. When he finished, Ritan nodded. "Thank you. As per FCM order, we have submitted your liaison to your legal system to do what you see fit."

Kraken nodded curtly, his tail still thrusting inside Eliza. "Thank you, Rit-tan. She will get what she deserve."

"Um, could I get a copy... of the video?"

"No." Kraken pulled his tail out of Eliza. It dripped with her juices as he tapped a button. A moment later, the screen sank back into the ground.

He turned to look at her. "Ritan does not like you."

Eliza peeled her hands away from her face. She shook her head, tears running down her cheeks. "He's going to have me executed... if you weren't already."

"Why would I?"

She stared at him. "What?"

"You defended yourself against an attack. There is no investigation, other than to find the rest of the family and eject them from the fleet. I will send them to the asteroid to seek shelter, otherwise they will die in space."

Her knees hit the ground. She barely registered the impact. "I-I didn't do wrong?"

Kraken bobbed through the water toward her. His tail slipped into the heated surface with a single ripple. When he reached her, he lifted his head and pressed his nose against her chin. "You were magnificent, like a hunter drenched in the blood of her prey."

She smiled. Without thinking, she wrapped her arms around his dripping head. "Thank you!"

His tail wrapped around her. "And, I will admit," he said in a low voice, "that excited me."

She giggled and kissed his head. "You like seeing me covered in blood?"

"Yes. Very much." A low rumble of his purr rippled the water.

"I bet the only thing you'd like better is watching me chase..." Her word died off as a memory welled up.

Kraken froze.

"Chase. You said everything was better when you chased it down."

The purring grew louder, a rumble that shook her body.

She stared at his bright blue, unblinking eye. Gulping, she felt a flicker of heat. "Is that how I can excite you? To make you harder?"

Her vision blurred from the intensity of his purr.

Eliza smiled, her pussy growing slick. "You want to hunt me and fuck me, don't you?"

It felt like holding a jackhammer in her hand. His entire body shook violently enough for the water to dimple and ripple.

"No," he rumbled.

She tensed, waiting for the words.

"I want to hunt you down and mate with you."

20 Genetics

She sat down heavily at the edge of the pool. "M-Mate?"

"Yes, mate. Breed, reproduce."

"But, we are completely different species."

"If you could, would you?"

Her body had grown slick and hot. The smell of her pussy wafted up to surround her. All her life, she was told she was flawed, an aberration that should have been trashed years before and the entire Midoze strain eliminated. And now, an alien wanted to breed her. Her, a throwback.

She looked up at him, tears burning her eyes and her breath coming in ragged gasps. "H-How? It isn't possible."

He held her close with his tail. "Not with genetics."

"But...?"

"Our species has secret when it comes to breeding. It is rooted in the need to show fitness, which is why I do not have a strong orgasm unless I hunt down my mate and breed her. It is usually forcible and there is frequently blood and screaming."

She moaned at the idea of being pinned by him, though the idea of being bitten tempered the edge of pleasure.

"It was not until later that the male remained to protect the female. That is why you met Billie's child but not the father. There are at least six for that many child."

Eliza thought about the swarm of young raptors, all of them blue with spotted yellow. "But, they look the same."

Kraken pulled back to look at her with one eye. "Yes, that is the other part. Our color, smell, and pattern," he gestured to his own crimson with yellow stripes, "come not from parentage, but with condition of nesting. Each family has a secret to their pattern, a secret that they will kill to protect. It is what identifies a Kraken from a Billie. And why your dress pattern was important to everyone."

She thought about the three dresses Billie had made. They were all yellow with red stripes, like Kraken's pattern but not quite. She looked over him. "But, I never saw another one like you before."

"No, because I am the last of the Kraken, and I have never mated. My six sibling were killed during the last ten jump. I am the last."

His tail dropped in the water, thumping against the surface.

She reached up and stroked his muzzle. "I'm sorry."

"Breeding is complicated. Exact chemical, temperature, and process. If anything go wrong, you get muddy color and a different pattern."

"But, couldn't you just say it was your own."

"I can, and many do, but the pattern is important. The color on this ship," he gestured to the cavern, "say I own it. This is Kraken's nest ship. Any creature without that pattern will find it hard to remain in control. The other would rebel."

She remember when she flew in and the massive ship had his coloration. It was hard to imagine a single raptor commanding the ship. She shivered and looked up at him. "The pattern is what keeps you in charge."

"Our species is bred to honor that color and nothing else."

She thought for a moment, staring down at the rippling water. "And you want to breed with me. How? I don't have your pattern or anything else."

"No, but your body has the right temperature for one step and the right chemicals. Not entirely, but I think you could carry the egg for a short period—"

Eliza gasped as she snapped her head up to stared at him. Her body pulsed with heat and hunger.

"—of time. It would be like mating, and you would contribute to their pattern. It won't be exact, but slight deviance are always acceptable. But, any child that come from your body would have the Kraken color."

"I... I..."

"I understand if you say no. Regardless of your answer, you are safe on this ship and welcome to stay aboard for the rest of your life, if you so choose. And I—"

"Yes!"

Kraken jumped at her scream.

Eliza blushed and pressed a hand against her belly. "Sorry, you don't understand. Before you, this womb would have never been used. We are born in tubes, a selection made by scientists and the admiralty. Our bodies, my sex, was considered a vestigial throwback to a more primitive time."

She was panting, her breasts rising and falling underneath her bandages. She rushed forward, unable to stop talking. "And then... then, you came into my life. I'm not a throwback for you. I'm not flawed or broken or damaged. You seem to like me for who I am, what I am. And, I would be honored to, at least pretend," she smiled, "to be a mother for your children."

For a long moment, she stared at him. Then, she giggled nervously. "Though, not so much biting if you're going to chase me down?"

Kraken lowered his head to her shoulder. He opened his mouth and playfully nipped her shoulder. "No more than that."

As a welcome surge of pleasure radiated from her shoulder, she smiled. "Maybe a little harder."

21 The Chase

Eliza panted as she vaulted over a ridge of rocks. Her bare feet slapped against a stone path, and she shot off along the textured stone. She dripped sweat, and heat boiled inside her. In the last week of healing, the injuries of her attack had faded into a finely-patterned texture of pink and scars. It was her own personal pattern, one that could never be duplicated.

Behind her, somewhere in a knot of artfully grown trees, Kraken roared. It was a brutal noise that filled the cavern and gave a promise of a violent coupling that would soon follow. Branches snapped as he charged forward, but she didn't dare look back.

She couldn't stop smiling. Her thighs were slick with sweat and her excitement. She wanted to stop and jam all her fingers into her cunt, but she couldn't. She would feel something inside her soon enough, her first cock, but first she had to make him work for it.

Seeing a bench, she jumped on it and then hopped over the stone ridge on the far side of the path. She followed it for a short distance, the sharp rocks cutting at her bare feet, before she grabbed a branch and swung down.

As soon as she struck the ground, she sprinted off. Leaves and vines whipped at her face and breasts, leaving scores against her skin, but adding to the anticipation.

A heavy thud and a crack of stone told her exactly where Kraken was. Only a few seconds away from catching her.

Eliza wanted to slow down, but that would ruin the moment. She had to fight right up to the end. He asked her to, begged actually. And her body screamed to give everything she could.

A tree cracked and she felt it thud against the ground. Not even the flying lizards burst out of the fallen branches; Kraken had ordered the cavern cleared of everything besides her and him.

She ran past a line of vendor's stalls. The meat and roasted vegetables still steamed along the trays. When he ordered the cavern empty for an hour, she didn't think it was enough. But, fifteen minutes in, she wondered if he could have done it in half the time.

Kraken roared again, his voice echoing against the stone walls as he sailed over her.

Eliza skidded to a halt as Kraken slammed into the ground in front of her. The stone shattered from the impact and shards flew in all directions. He spun around and roared again, the blast of air washing over her.

Her eyes drifted down and she gasped. He was hard. Harder than she thought possible. A meter-length cock, red and bloody, bobbed from his crotch. It was already drooling, leaving behind wet splatters of clear liquid as Kraken took a step toward her.

His growl sent quivers of pleasure coursing along her body. Her knees threatened to buckle as she saw the enraged, and excited, raptor chasing her. His claws dug into the rock and his tail curled clear up to his head.

She spun around and sprinted back the other way, heading toward the vendor carts again. She reached the nearest one and jumped over it, her hand planted on the still hot heating element.

As she landed, she spotted an iron pole used to mark the line for the vendor. Inspiration grew and she grabbed it when she passed. It was heavy with a large base. On the next cart, she slammed it down and snapped off the base to give her a weapon similar to the one she used to kill the smaller raptors.

Kraken hit the first cart and she heard the faux wood snapping as he charged through it. A hunk of meat and a chunk of sparking electronics flew over her head.

She almost came from the intoxicating mix of fear and excitement. He was fast, faster than anything she could imagine. But, it wasn't death that would come when he caught her. He was going to impale her on his massive cock and use her body the way evolution intended.

Her pussy spasmed with her thoughts. She stumbled with the intensity before crawling over the rock marker and off the trail. The stone scraped her nipples, adding to the tiny cuts and scratches from her run, but she didn't care. It was just foreplay now.

She scanned the plants around her, looking for a soft place for her last stand. When she spotted a large, moss-covered rock, she turned and headed toward it.

Kraken's head slammed into her back, shooting her forward. She let out a scream as she thumped against the rock. The soft, spongy plant broke her fall but the impact drove the air briefly from her lungs.

Trying to pant, she spun around and swung her weapon. It cracked against the side of Kraken's head and he staggered to the side.

Eliza froze, worried that she had gone too far.

A splatter of cum blasted against her. Kraken growled, a low rumbling sound as he brought his head back to her. He was drooling and shaking from the intensity of his growling.

Relieved, she swung again.

This time, Kraken grabbed her wrist with one large claw and clamped down. Pricks of pain slashed through her senses as she stared at him. Muscles bulged underneath his crimson skin and he pulled her up.

Eliza whimpered, suddenly afraid that Kraken was going to do more than just mate with her. She cried out and used her free hand to grab at his claw.

Kraken opened his grip and grabbed her other hand. With a snarl, he clamped down on her and lifted her completely off the ground.

The tension in her shoulders burst across her senses. She kicked out helplessly, caught in his grip. Her nerves were on fire and her pussy pulsed with desperation. She didn't know if she was going to die or orgasm in the moment.

Kraken's tail snapped out, cracking against her thighs.

She screamed out wordlessly. Her twists in his grip made her feel more like prey with every passing second.

The tail came back and she tensed for another crack, but he wrapped around her left leg and pulled it up. Her leg strained to keep her balance, but she felt her nether entrance spreading open.

Looking down her sweat-slicked body, she saw his dripping cock aiming to penetrate her. She sobbed with need, trying to fight her way through the storm of desire, lust, and fear.

He thrust forward. His crimson cock speared into her, ripping her pussy open and filling her with a single thrust. His body jerked as he stopped just as quickly, with only a third of his length buried in her sex.

Eliza froze. She had never felt such as heat inside her; it seemed to pulse and burn her from the inside. The sensation of being filled was nothing compared to her fingers or random tools from her room. It was hot and living, slick and hard.

She tried to clamp down, to push out the unfamiliar intruder, but her body couldn't eject him. Instead, it just added to the intensity of having something filling her to the brim.

Kraken's tail released her leg and she felt her weight focusing on the cock buried inside her. The massive intruder spread her further than she thought possible.

When his tip thumped against her cervix, he grabbed her with his free claw and relieved the pressure. Drawing his hips back, Kraken wrapped his tail around his cock, creating a knot that identified the limits of her body.

She barely had time to comprehend what he was doing when he drove back into her. His cock drove deep into her cunt, stretching it widely open. An explosion of pleasure rocketed through her body, and she clamped down on the searing length.

Kraken withdrew his cock and drove it home again. His tail punched against her labia, stopping his length from tearing her open. The impact, wet and slick, felt like a slap, and she arched her back in her helplessness.

Eliza tried to pull her hands free of his grip, but he held her too tightly. She couldn't move, caught between her wrists and cunt. With every thrust of his hips, she screamed out and felt her body spasm with an orgasm that never seemed to end.

The raptor threw her down against the moss. The soft rock caught her. She started to slide off his length, but he grabbed her breasts with both claws. The sharp points scraped against her skin, leaving red lines that began to well blood.

She writhed on his hardness, caught by the pistoning cock that drove with hard, brutal strokes. She reached out for him, unsure if she was going to push him away or grab him.

Kraken answered by catching her hands with his mouth. Sharp teeth broke skin along her arms and wrist.

She couldn't move except to writhe helplessly. The claws on her breasts, the teeth on her wrists, and the girth that stretched her gloriously open was too much to handle. She screamed out as the orgasm tore through her, ripping along her senses in sharp waves of white-hot pleasure.

He continued to drive into her, a rapid fire stroke that felt more mechanical than organic. Punch after punch filled her to her limits. The wet slurping of their combined juices poured out of her opening, soaking her thighs before puddling on the ground beneath him.

His thrusts grew faster and harder. The impact of his body against her own pushed her right to the edge of pleasure and pain. It hurt, but every punch against her insides also drove waves of pleasure throughout her body.

With a roar, he released her wrists and drove deep into her. His orgasm was a blast of thick semen. It seared her insides as the high-pressure spurt filled in her in an instant. It shot out of her body, squelching as long streamers of cream burst out from her abused sex. She felt it swelling around his cock, an ache of her body straining to contain something that no human had ever been bred for.

Eliza didn't slump back, the muscles of her belly tightened as she reached up to clutch his neck. She felt her own orgasms adding to the searing sensation of being bred, filled.

He continued to roar, driving her completely off the rock with his final thrusts. His claws scraped down her side as he grabbed her thighs and forced them apart. Sharp points of his tips pierced her skin.

More cum continued to blast out of her, but he withdrew with each stroke. She felt the empty feeling left behind by his massive cock fill with thick cum. It was almost solid, like paste. It filled her pussy completely and prevented the strained walls from relaxing.

He slipped out with his final blast, splattering her pussy, stomach, and breasts with his semen. She slumped, but his claws caught her. With a growl, he pulled her up from the rock.

Eliza moaned as her head slipped off the moss and swung underneath. She was held upside down, her abused pussy being brought up to his mouth. Panting and moaning, she watched as he stared down at her with his bright eye.

A thud filled the air. She glanced around to see Hissa coming up, her head bowed. In her hand was a bucket.

Kraken reached into the bucket with his tail. When he pulled back, there was a speckled egg the side of her fist.

Eliza moaned. She was about to be bred.

When he pressed the egg against her entrance, she thought it would hurt. But the thick cum and her stretched open hole accepted the alien egg. With a surprisingly gentle touch, he pushed it inside and she felt it sinking through the thickening cum.

Globs of semen rolled down her body as he added a second egg into her pussy, gently guiding it into her splayed open lips. She shuddered at the feeling of something hard and smooth settling inside her tunnel.

"One more?" he panted.

Eliza opened her mouth and then whimpered. She felt full, more full than she ever had. She didn't want to squeeze down, but her body did. As it did, she felt the hardness buried inside her, forcing her open as more cum squelched out.

"No more." He reached down and lapped at her sex. The draw of his tongue against her aching clitoris sent after-tremors of pleasure. Almost instantly, she felt the semen harden into a thick clot of cum.

With a gentle movement, Kraken pulled her right side up and clutched her to his chest. "Thank you," he rumbled.

She shuddered at the sensation of being filled. Closing her eyes, she rested her head against his head. She was exhausted, both in body and sex. She had been bred by an alien, and it left her aching.

As she began to drift to sleep, she felt him carrying her away. They were going to a private birthing ship, the Kraken's most secret of places where she would eventually release the eggs to join the legacy of the master of the fleet.

With a smile, she let the darkness take her.

22 Waking Up

Eliza moaned as she clawed her way out of unconsciousness. Or at least she thought she did. It was hard to identify her body, her voice, or even her thoughts with the clutching darkness mulling in her consciousness. It felt like she was being pulled down into a choking abyss, a world where she would never wake up if she fell.

Her eyelids fluttered, but she couldn't break the seal of dried tears. She focused on her legs. They moved, but a pressure ground down on them. Every time she strained, it felt as if they were sliding through a thick muck. It exhausted her quickly, and she still felt trapped.

Without having an idea of where she was, Eliza focused her attention on her arms. They were above her, she could tell from the tension in her shoulders and back, but when she tugged on them, they didn't move. Instead, a metallic clink rose up through her foggy senses. Tilting her head, she jerked her arms again. The rattling increased, as did pressure along her arms.

A pounding filled her ears, shaking the world for a moment before stopping. "You are awake."

She almost sobbed at Kraken's voice. "K-Kraken? I can't see you."

Her chain rattled and then she felt his tongue against her face. It was rough and gentle, working along her eyes before lapping at her throat.

She tilted her head up to give him access, the knowledge that she willing bared her throat adding a dull throb of pleasure deep inside.

Eliza frowned; she felt her body responding. There was a pressure inside her, a hardness that had never been there before. At first, she thought it was from his cock buried inside her, but it didn't have

141

the pulsating heat or slickness. Instead, it was a constant touch at exactly her body's temperature.

She brought her legs together, forcing them through the resistance. As she moved, the pressure inside her depths increased. After a few seconds, she relaxed her legs.

Kraken pulled back. "Open your eye, it is dim in here."

Forcing her eyes open, she stared at the blurry images until she could focus on Kraken's crimson head and blue eyes. "W-What," her voice cracked, "happened?"

His tail wagged back and forth. "You exhausted yourself, and the mating put your system into shock from an unexpected allergic response. We stabilized you, but the drugs had some unexpected side effect. You passed out, so I brought you to my nest ship."

Images of the massive fleet ship drifted through her mind. "The nest ship? Weren't we already there?"

"No, this is a smaller private one. Locked and defended against intruder. This is my secret place."

She smiled, the fog in her head was clearing, "The place for your pattern?"

"Yes."

Eliza lifted her head and peered at her wrist. She was naked, that part she knew, but someone had put on soft, leather cuffs that went from the base of her thumb to her elbow. The inside was soft, like Kraken's belly, but the outside had a large strap that ended with a hook.

At the moment, the hooks from both arms were attached to a large ring. It didn't appear to be binding her in place, she could easily pull herself off by grabbing the hooks and twisting.

Confused, she looked down at the resistance surrounding her body. She was tits deep in a thick, almost black, muck. It lapped at her nipples and coated her skin from her movements. She could feel it rolling against her bare buttocks, legs, and even up between her legs. But, despite her legs naturally separating in the muck, she felt none of it sliding into her pussy. There was something there, a pressure that refused to relent.

She looked up. "The eggs! Are they okay?"

Kraken purred and nodded. He turned so his nose pressed against her cheek. "They are perfect and healthy."

Eliza leaned against his head, trapped in the rings and muck. With a grin, she glanced up and down. "This is kind of... compromising, isn't it?"

"I," he chuckled, "did the best I could. The mud is actually slurry of chemicals, all natural, but from my ancestor homeland. You need to be submerged inside it when the plug dissolve in many day. Otherwise, the coloration will change with exposure to oxygen."

He gestured with his tail toward the edge of the stone pool. There was a pile of pillows, some rope and chains, and even a cushion. All of them covered in muck. Beyond, she saw her clothes and weapons sitting on an alcove. "I had some trouble keeping you safe when I cannot be here."

"Thank you," she grinned, "it would be bad if I drowned."

"Very bad, might ruin the pattern." But, his dead-panned seriousness was interrupted by the playful quiver of his tail.

"Yeah," she said and leaned against her stretched arm. "That would be terrible." At least her position didn't hurt, only ached a little.

Curious, she scanned the room. She was in a muck-filled pool about six meters long by three meters. Her position was at the far end of the room, the furthest from the archway leading to the rest of the ship. The entire room was nothing but a stone cavern, though she guessed the stone was artificial and, no doubt, filled with sensors. She saw murals of red raptors covering the walls. All of them had blue eyes and yellow strips along their back.

"You are safe here, but I cannot remain."

"Duties?"

"Yes, I must go back to the asteroid to start my end game. We are about to go our separate ways."

Eliza nodded and bobbed her head. "I can get off this?"

"Yes, but do not leave the mud. I do not have a detail analysis of the chemicals in your sex. The plug could dissolve sooner than I plan, though I think it will not."

"S-Should I grab the eggs?"

"No, they will sink to the bottom. This is where they need to belong, covered completely and safe from oxygen and cold. Also, the mud protect against pressure changes."

She took a deep breath and lifted her wrist. The metal of the hook scraped as she slipped off it. Her body sank into the mud faster than she expected. With a yelp, she grabbed the ring tightly.

Kraken's tail snapped out, holding above her hand. "Careful, do not drown." His voice rumbled with concern.

Eliza panted as she hooked her arm back on the ring. She felt vulnerable and helpless, but she wasn't ready to swim on her own. When the hook snapped into place, she slumped down.

Kraken's tail snapped back and forth. "Are you safe?"

"Your eggs are safe."

"I did not ask about eggs, I asked about you. Is Eliza safe?"

She lifted her gaze up to him. "Yes."

"Good, because an egg can be replaced, you cannot."

She smiled, a blush rising on her cheeks. "Thank you."

"Thank you. You have given me great joy in these month. I cannot thank you enough. You have," he grinned, "made me very curious."

"Me too."

"Rest. Your body can handle your position and you are safe. I will come back in one day time. But, after that, it will be six. The automated system," he gestured to a blinking control panel, "will ensure you are fed and clean."

"Um, what if I have to go the bathroom?"

Kraken leaned down. "You have many tube in your hole. You are safe and well taken care of."

"You mean," she stared at him, "I won't have to eat either?"

"No, that was required. I promise, when you get out, we have a proper dinner."

"With chasing?"

His tail whipped faster. "There will be many types of chasing after this."

"Good." Eliza slumped back and closed her eyes. She was exhausted from her ordeal.

She listened to Kraken's thumps as he circled the room and headed for the door.

Just as she started to lose track of it, a thought cut through her exhaustion. "Kraken?" she cried.

He came back. "Yes?"

"If the fleet is jumping," she gulped, "what is going to happen to me?"

Kraken stepped back into the room, his head bobbing. "Do you wish to return to the FCM *Quantor*?"

"No, but—"

"You have been assigned to us via our laws. You are a citizen of the fleet ship now, not the asteroid. If you wish, and I hope you do, you are welcome to join me when we jump to the next, very random, point in the universe. You will never see the asteroid again."

She relaxed. "Thank you."

"As I said, I'm looking forward to an opponent. It just happens that you are it, and I desperately hope you will challenge me for many year to come."

Kraken padded around to press his chin to her cheek. "Sleep, Eliza. You are safe here, I promise."

23 Dreams

There was something peaceful about being dangled into a pool of chemical slime. She had no worries to dwell on her thoughts. The temperature of the pool matched her own body, and she had no sensation of being cold, hot, or anything besides held.

She dragged her legs through the muck just to feel the ripples of the thick slime. Her pussy, now accustomed to the pressure of the eggs, squeezed down on the curved hardness inside her. It was comforting to be filled, though occasionally her body grew warm when the movement reminded her of Kraken's cock driving deep inside her.

Wrapping her hands around the ring, she pulled herself up and off the hooks. The metal thumped against her wrist before she lowered herself deeper into the thick slime. She could feel it tugging her down; the pressure and currents were a challenge at first, but now she swirled her arms and kicked her legs slowly, bobbing in the thick liquid before swimming slowly toward the far end.

As she swam, she felt the pressure of the two tubes, the one impaling her ass and a catheter. She still didn't know how Kraken got them in, but the automated system ensured she was fed, though not through her mouth, and the slime retained its chemical properties.

She sighed. It would take her a few days to get used to not being in the pool when she finally left.

Splatters of muck hit her face with one stroke, but she didn't bother wiping it off. She was covered in the stuff from head to toe. It wasn't dangerous, she knew that, but it also tasted acidic and horrid.

Reaching the far end, she planted her feet on the bottom of the pool. The surface was slick and sloped. She started to slide back, but she clutched the side and bobbed down. Rolling over, she brought her body up to the surface, not quite breaking it but enough to see the slime bulging up.

With her other hand, she stroked along her belly. There was a firm hardness right above her hips. It wasn't pregnancy, she didn't even know if her body could handle it after seventy-three generations of genetic manipulation, but she could pretend it was her own child growing inside her.

Her palm caressed her soft, smooth skin. Her scars had softened in the muck until she could barely feel them. Below the curve of the two eggs bulging out, the hardened plug of semen continued to hold her tight together.

She stroked her pubic mound with her fingertips, trying to find the little strands of hair. She didn't know when she lost her hair, but something in the muck had removed them. When she finally left, she would find out if they would grow back or if she would become hairless like the raptor she loved.

With a smile, she leaned back and held on the edge of the pool. Three days until Kraken came back from the asteroid. In her mind, the FCM *Quantor* wasn't home anymore. It was just a place where the other humans lived.

Her smile grew. She wasn't going back, ever.

Splaying her legs, she let the pool tug her down until only her head remained above the surface. Her knuckles ached to hold her, but the rest of her felt relaxed and liquid. If she was bred again, she would ask for rings along the entire length of the pool. That way she could change positions over the two weeks of waiting for the plug to dissolve.

A metallic bang vibrated the ground.

Eliza slowly opened her eyes and watched the slow ripples crossing the pool.

Another bang, this one stronger, shook the ground and more ripples coursed along the surface.

She frowned. Kraken wasn't due for three days, and he said no one would be on the ship. The unexpected sound sent a prickle of concern through her. Though she rarely felt it, the timing sounded uncomfortably familiar like a ship docking. She thought for a moment and held her breath, waiting for double chunk of the universal bracket snapping into place.

It was the faintest of vibrations and a set of double ripples sluggishly raced across the pool that told her someone was docking against Kraken's nest ship. She felt her breath quickening even as she hoped it was Kraken coming sooner than expected.

She waited for his tell-tale thuds, but there was nothing.

Time seemed to slow down around her as she strained to listen for anything to indicate her lover had returned. Her imagination played tricks on her, making her hear beeps and rustles that didn't exist. As she held herself still, her pulse began to beat in her ears, obscuring any sounds.

She was trapped in the pool. What was peaceful a few seconds ago was now a prison. She panted and pulled herself half out of the liquid, keeping the muck lapping at her hips. Her breasts, soft and pale, ground against the sharp rocks as she turned and settled down.

Eliza stared at the archway, waiting for something.

At the first thud, she let out a sigh of relief.

A second didn't come.

She held her breath again, but it wasn't a thud that echoed down the hall but a scrape of a metal and a beeping noise.

Fear slammed into her, coursing through her veins.

Then the beeping grew louder, as if someone was typing into a control panel. It was a fast, tinny noise that echoed down the tunnels of the ship.

Eliza reached down with her free hand, over her hip, and grabbed the tube that impaled her ass. Something was wrong and she needed to be free. She hesitated as she wrapped her fingers around the thick implement. Kraken said that she had to be immersed in case the plug dissolved. The eggs couldn't survive the cold or the oxygen; she was in danger. Slowly, she unwrapped her fingers and dipped into the pool.

The beeping continued for a second, then a mechanical voice drifted into the room. "Proximity mine has been armed." It was a female's voice, but one that Eliza had heard before. The sound came from a series of mines, grenades, and bombs that every crew member of the asteroid had to practice with. The only difference is that she didn't hear the word "simulated" before the announcement.

Footsteps followed and then more beeping.

Eliza grabbed the tube in her ass with a firm grip. Eggs or not, she couldn't stay inside. Someone was in the ship and it was human.

She had never had something in her rectum before, and she was unconscious when Kraken managed to feed it in. Gripping the side of the pool tightly, she tugged on it. She felt the pressure increase inside her bowels but the tube refused to move. With a whimper, she pulled harder. The sensation of her anus stretching brought a wave of discomfort to course through her system.

Her body trembling, she gripped harder and pushed down. A flared tip of the tube bulged out of her. She wanted to scream out at the discomfort, but that would give away her position. Instead, she sobbed into her hand and pulled it out.

The base of the tube popped out of her ass and she spasmed. Her sphincter clamped down on the part still inside her. Staring at the archway through the tears, she pulled it out of her. It was longer than she expected, and she felt every millimeter that wound into her organs as she drew it out of her aching ass.

When the last of it came out and her sphincter tightened on nothing but her own flesh, she let out a gasp of relief.

The catheter took less effort, but wasn't any less comfortable.

She dragged both tubes out of the slime and set them down on the side. The plastic scraped against the rock, slipping back until the tips caught on a edge.

Eliza winced at the sound and glanced fearfully at the archway. No FCM soldier came rushing in, but they were setting a third proximity mine. Pulling up her memories, she thought about the options of the mines. She guessed whoever was there was setting them to exploded when a large creature passed within two meters. It would be the safest option for a small human compared to a six meter long raptor.

She struggled with her choices, but the looming danger finally pushed her out of the pool. One hand clamped against her sex and the plug, she crawled out on the rocks. The air was moist and warm, but she still trembled with fear for the eggs.

Staggering to her feet, it took a moment to gain her balance. Then, she padded around the pool back to her clothes and weapon. She felt strange walking bow-legged and with her palm against her sex, but the idea that the eggs would come out right at the worst time kept playing through her mind.

She reached the alcove with tears running down her cheeks. She wanted to throw herself back in the pool and pray no one would find her, but she knew that a FCM operative would be more than competent enough to see a single human in a pool.

Even if she managed to escape, Kraken would be killed as soon as he came to her.

She fumbled with the clothes before she realized it was her shredded dress. The fabric had been torn and there was blood on the edges. It wouldn't fit over her, even for a few steps, before fluttering off.

Fear burning brightly, she grabbed her weapon and checked the charge. It was full. Switching it to vibrating feedback, she leaned against the wall and stared at the arch.

She had one hand against her pussy and her gun in the other. Her entire body was covered in muck but it was slowly sliding down over her naked breasts and along her trembling thighs.

A flash of hope rose up. Whoever looked inside may be startled by her appearance enough to get off a shot. She wouldn't have much of a chance against a better trained opponent, but she was a Midoze. There were very few genetic strands that bred better shots than her.

Footsteps drifted through the archway. The operative was drawing closer.

She gulped and aimed her gun at the arch. Her breath came faster and harder, scraping against her throat with every rise of her chest. Her fingers clutched her opening, praying that the eggs wouldn't push out.

Soon, she could hear the sharp edge of a tactical boot against the stone ground. It shot out with every step, sounding like a rifle report.

Eliza double-checked the safety and held her finger lightly on the trigger. She didn't know what side of the invader would approach, so she kept her gun aimed at the center.

A spasm rippled her insides and she felt the eggs shifting.

Fear burned bright, and she gripped her opening tighter, pinching at the thick mass blocking the eggs from escaping. She inched toward the pool, lowering herself in preparation of slipping inside.

There was a flash of black. The operative stepped into the arch and looked inside. They wore a tactical uniform, pitch black with a wide, glass face shield that gave no hint of the person inside. The armor was thicker than her flight suit and capable of taking an energy weapon at close range. But, she knew the armor's weakness. There was a small, one centimeter wide seal right at the neck that didn't have the same protection as the rest.

In their hands was PR-31, a short-range plasma rifle suited for close combat and rapid fire. It easily had ten times the force of her own pistol and twenty times the charge. With only slime protecting her, she would be killed by the first shot.

Eliza moved automatically, aiming and firing. But, as her finger depressed the trigger, she recognize a small pistol hanging in a holster of the operative. It was the same as the one in her hands.

She was firing at her brother.

She twitched and the plasma shot splashed harmlessly off the operative's shoulder.

A flash of heat rolled back her as the shelf behind her ignited into a flames. The stench of plasma surrounded her.

She shook her head. "No, not you, Duncan."

The operative froze. "Eliza?"

Eliza knew that he identified her. There was no way he would have missed even with the distance of the pool. He was stalling.

She didn't have time, not with the eggs beginning to slide down. The pressure in her sex had lessened, and she could feel thick globs of drying cum oozing between her fingers before splattering to the ground beneath her. "I have to get back in the pool."

"No," said Duncan. "Ritan reported you as killed in action." His gun never wavered.

"I was attacked."

"You murdered people... those things." His voice lost his humanity with his helmet on, but she knew he wouldn't take it off. She could only imagine his black hair and brown eyes. And hope that he was hesitating at least a little.

"It was self-defense."

"Why didn't you report back?"

"Ritan wanted me dead, Kraken made him think it happened."

He tilted his shoulder back, giving less of a shot and rotating the weak helmet seal away from her. "That's treason, Eliza. They'll execute you for that."

She looked him over, trying to find some way of winning this fight. The globs of cum were pouring out of her faster. She tried to palm her sex, but it only slowed down the flow. She could almost count the seconds before the eggs were ruined forever.

To her surprise, she considered the distance to the pool. Her brother would shoot her, but then the eggs would be safe. She could picture herself dying with the eggs slipping safely to the bottom. And wondered if she would feel peace.

She stepped closer.

"Don't move, Eliza. I'm a better shot than you."

With a nod, she glanced down at the pool. "I know, Duncan, but I have to get back in there."

"Why?"

"I can't... I can't tell you." Her body spasmed and her pussy clamped down on the eggs. The first one shifted and began to slip out of her.

Eliza wanted to take another step, but she couldn't. Her survival instinct rose up, righting her desire. Tears ran down her cheeks as she struggled against her own need to live. When a huge surge of cum poured out from her fingers, she gasped. "I have to! I can't lose these eggs!"

"Eggs?"

Tears welled in her eyes. "K-Kraken's."

She heard him inhale. "You really are flawed."

"There is nothing wrong with me!"

"You copulated with a raptor! Humans don't have sex. They don't let their base drives run their lives. There is something wrong with you. And if you think some alien's eggs are more important than your life, then I will kill you before you touch the water... dirt, whatever that stuff is!"

Eliza shook her head. Her hand wavered but the muzzle of her pistol remained trained on her brother. "No, I can't let you."

"Would you," his voice grew quieter, "really die to save some creature's eggs?"

"Y-Yes. Yes, I would. Haven't you ever done something you felt was right but everyone else told you was wrong?"

"No, I'm a soldier." Unlike her gun, his remained steady as rock. "I do not question."

"Aren't you...?" She sobbed for the words. "Weren't you ever curious about anything?"

"No." His gun shivered once. "Damn it, Eliza, why did you have to be passionate about this, of all things? He isn't one of us. He isn't human."

"Because I love him!" It spilled out before she realized it.

"Love? You love Kraken?"

She nodded. "More than anything else. I... I want to stay here, with him. I don't want to go back. I don't want to be part of the FCM anymore."

The opening of her sex began to swell with the egg coming out. She could feel the thick layer of Kraken's cum still protecting it, but she only had moments before it was exposed to the air.

She sobbed. "Duncan, you have to let me do this." She shook her weapon. "Please don't make me shoot my own brother."

"I'm a better shot and I'm faster."

"I won't miss, this is too important to me."

His head lowered slightly, and he twisted. She saw his tactical pack come into view. If he only set three or four of the proximity mines, there would be two more inside. She focused on the latch.

Duncan's voice echoed across the pool. "I won't either, Eliza."

A sense of wrongness filled her. Duncan would have never exposed a vulnerability to her. He was too much of a soldier. She trembled and tensed, she had to get back to the pool.

Then Duncan's voice came in a whisper. "Don't miss."

She wasn't sure she heard it at first, but then it came again.

"Don't miss, sister."

She sobbed as she fired twice. The first blew the latch off the tactical pack. As it swung open, she angled a shot to bounced off the inside of the hard shell. The blast of plasma ricocheted off the pack, snapping it off, but then punched into his back.

The mines didn't go off, but Duncan staggered forward. His own gun smoking from his shot, but she couldn't afford to feel her injuries.

Eliza braced herself and waited the split second as the helmet seal came into view. She fired once, knowing she couldn't miss.

The helmet exploded as the plasma punched though the vulnerable latch and burned through her brother's neck. He was dead before he hit the ground.

She sobbed and ran for the pool, dropping her weapon to clutch herself. She dove in, curling up as the warm muck swallowed her.

The first egg slipped out from her fingers. She caressed it as it passed, marveling at the textured surface. It tumbled off her fingers and into the depths of the pool, where it would be safe until Kraken came.

She kicked to surface, careful not to touch the bottom to avoid crushing the egg. The second came out just as she surfaced. She felt it slipping out of her sex, straining her labia, and scraping against the cut she got from the raptor attack.

Eliza tried to reach for it, but it slipped free before her fingers could caress it. She sobbed and gasped for air, the sharp taste of the muck burning her tongue. With one hand, she wiped her face clear and stared fearfully at the entrance, expecting to see a squad of assassins waiting for her.

There was nothing.

Trembling from a sudden exhaustion, she crawled out of the pool and along the ground. She came up to her brother and fumbled with his helmet. Tears splashed down, mixing with the dark mud, and splashed on his armor.

She pulled it free. At the sight of his plasma burned face, the tears came faster. "No, Duncan, why?"

But, there was no answer.

Gasping, she inspected her body. Her fingers scraped off the muck while she tried to find where he shot her. There was no way he missed, not a Midoze, not Duncan. But, after long moments of searching, she knew he didn't hit her.

She trembled as she looked back at the pool. At the far end, a meter away from where she stood, was a single smoking blast hole. Duncan had struck the eye of the raptor in the mural, a precise shot that left a perfect circle of a bright blue eye.

He didn't miss.

He just chose not to hit her.

Enemy Mine

Eliza forced herself off Duncan's body. Panting, she stared into his burnt face for a moment, then flipped him over. She found the plasma burst from where she shot him in the back, but there were no mines in the tactical pack.

Duncan had set them up before he found her.

"Damn you," she whispered. With a shaking hand, she pulled his custom pistol from his holster. It was a gift from her, a year's worth of saving her requisition points to order it. It was identical to her own, down to the design on the muzzle.

Returning to the pool, she picked up her gun, holster, and the remains of her dress. The gun went around her waist, hanging against her naked hip. She took Duncan's weapon and wrapped it in the dress. She wasn't sure what she would do with it, but she couldn't leave it behind.

She left Duncan's body where it fell. There was nothing she could do about him and she didn't know if she was still in danger. Her bare feet slapped against the stone as she worked her way along the side of the tunnel. She remembered her gun and went back, strapping the holster over her muck-slicked hip and drawing the weapon.

Her first priority was to find the mines. She didn't have the codes to deactivate them, that would have been set by military intelligence. But, everyone on the asteroid knew the code to reveal the parameters that would trigger an explosion.

As she approached the first one, she felt sick. Her feet slowed as she came up to it. The mine was a flat disc, about three centimeters thick and ten across. It appeared to be featureless but she blew gently on it until the thermal-sensitive display swam into view. Reaching up with a trembling hand, she tapped in the reveal code.

A swirl of information flashed on the screen. She flipped through the menus until to bring up the intelligence programming. It took her a moment to translate the settings. The mines were programmed to trigger whenever an organic creature over three hundred kilograms approached. The explosive charge was high enough to vaporize Kraken and most of the ship hull behind him.

She swore underneath her breath and continued down the hall. Each of the mines were programmed the same: to destroy Kraken.

The nest ship was remarkably small, a medium-classed freighter at most. It took her a depressingly little time to investigate the corridors. There was nothing for her to wear or even wrap around her naked body, not unless she wanted to punch out the bottom of a bucket. She sighed and padded around again, trying to find anything.

The interior of the ship had been made up to look like tunnels. She wondered if the textured walls were similar to his ancestral home. It may have been peaceful and soothing for Kraken, but the decorations left little in terms of weapons, supplies, or anything else.

She fought her fear as she circled the ship around again. Besides the pool, a locked door to the cockpit, and the standard airlock, there was nothing. Desperate, she headed into the airlock. The large transparent shield gave a stunning view of the endless black of space.

Eliza sighed and pressed her forehead against the shield. She was trapped in the ship, but at least she was safe. If she could get to Kraken before he walked past the airlock.

Her eyes opened and she pushed herself away from the shield. Duncan would have set the first mines in the lock, it was standard procedure. A feeling of discomfort prickled her skin but she couldn't find it.

And then she looked up. The last two mines were mounted along the ceiling, hidden from sight by a grill missing a screw. But, the familiar polished disk was obvious from her position on the ground. It wouldn't be for a raptor entering his sanctuary.

"Damn you, Duncan, you really were the best."

She sank down to the ground. Exhausted, she dragged at her limbs with every effort to crawl to the pressure door. Her only hope was to warn Kraken before he entered the airlock. She didn't know if she could do it in time, but she had to try.

25 Rescued

The high-pitch screen of the airlock ripped her out of her dreams. Eliza stood up straight, scraping her back along the textured wall. Her legs trembled with the effort to remain standing.

With a hiss, the pressure door came swinging down. The heavy steel settled into place with a thud, and then the shudder of four bolts slamming into place.

Eliza peered through the porthole as the ship came into view. It was bright blue with yellow splotches along the bottom: Billie's ship. The freighter docked with unsurprising grace and the familiar thuds of two massive crafts locking together.

Her heart pounding faster as she shifted from one foot to another. Her naked breasts bounced with her movements and flakes of dried mud cascaded to the ground. She stared at the porthole, silently hoping that Kraken wouldn't charge forward into the airlock and set off the mines.

The agonizing wait for the air to pressurize tore at her. She bit her lip and tugged at the handle, as if she could move a metal door a hundred times her weight. She whimpered and tugged faster. "Come on. Come on!"

When the door finally started to rise, she grabbed the edge and yanked with her might. Icy wind blasted her as she strained to make enough space for her to slip through. As soon as she could, she ground herself into the cold metal and slipped through.

On the far side, she staggered to her feet. "Don't come in!"

"Eliza?" it was Billie.

"Billie! Don't let Kraken in!"

The tiny blue raptor stood in the entrance of her ship. "Kraken? He is not here. I was worried about you."

Stunned, Eliza stopped in the middle. "Me?"

"Yes, I saw there were two FCM ship flying around. One docked. It looked strange because the communication system is out and they were not landing on the nest ship. As soon as they take off, I circle around and dock."

Billie stepped forward, her tiny claws ticking against the metal surface of the airlock. "Are you okay?"

Eliza shivered and clutched herself, the memories welled up. "I had to kill my brother."

The raptor's head and tail drooped. "I'm sorry. One should never kill sibling. Family is everything."

Unable to speak, Eliza nodded.

"Are the egg safe?"

"In the pool, but we have to warn Kraken. There are proximity mines set to explode when he approaches."

"But, safe to us?"

"Yes, but..." Her voice trailed off. Billie had one eye tilted at her, the bright yellow regarding her. There was no way to see emotions in the unblinking yellow. Eliza's eyes darted to Billie's tail. It didn't move from its drooped expression of sadness. "But, I'm not sure for how long. We have to tell Kraken."

Billie bobbed her head in agreement. "Then we leave. Right now. If we hurry, we can get within short range in an hour. Then you talk to him."

Fighting a niggling discomfort, Eliza nodded. "Please?"

"Of course. We lock the ship up tight and leave. No one come and steal the egg, right?"

Eliza nodded. Turning around, she grabbed her dress and the gun inside it before following Billie into the raptor's ship. She was thankful Billie showed no sign of wanting to explore the ship or question her anymore, but something prickled against her senses. She wasn't sure if it was paranoia or something else, but she kept remembering how Kraken said his kind would kill over family patterns.

Inside Billie's ship, Eliza started up toward the cockpit but stopped. She had to find out for sure. Turning around, she made a show of looking at the mud caked to her body. "Ug, I don't want to mess up your ship. Do you have a shower on-board?"

Billie's tail snapped up and her head bobbed. "Oh yes. I have a small nest in the far back. There is a steam shower. Small, but you might fit in there. I do not have clothes, though. I didn't think I'd be picking up naked human today."

Eliza grinned, but didn't feel it. The second of wrongness continued to pluck at her senses. She padded down the narrow corridor to Billie's nest.

It was a small sleeping quarters, but similar in arrangement Kraken's. The center of the room had a circular indention filled with round cushions of dozens of different colors. Little alcoves were filled with entertainment balls, pictures, and knickknacks from Billie's hundred young.

Crawling on the cushions, Eliza looked for a computer display. She knew it was hidden, like most of the equipment on the nest ship. After a few moments of poking around a promising ridge, she managed to find the release for the display. It rose up with a hiss, images flashing across the screen.

They were pictures of Billie's children. One flashed up of a pair of raptors fighting over a bit of string. Another one of Eliza buried underneath the swarm; she was laughing and flailing as the tiny raptors jumped her. A third of five raptors curled up in a nest, each one a different color. The images continued to randomly appear to the screen.

Eliza tapped the screen to stop the show and flipped through the menus. The language was still unfamiliar to her, but she knew enough to find the external sensors and bring up the cameras. Flipping through it, she found one that showed Kraken's nest ship rapidly shrinking with distance.

The ship was plain-looking. It didn't have Kraken's customary pattern. It wasn't even red, but simply glistening metal and black paint. The only identification was a serial number in the sharp script of the raptors.

Relief flooded through her. No one would know to investigate the ship. There was nothing to indicate it held Kraken's most private secret. She only hoped her eggs would remain safe until she could tell Kraken.

Tapping the screen to stop the video, Eliza leaned back on her knees. She stared at the screen, trying to figure out why she was worried.

Unable to come up with anything, she sighed. "I'm just worried."

But the feeling never stopped. She started to crawl out of the nest but then decided to cater to her paranoia. Taking her gun, she shoved it deep into the circular cushions before folding the tattered remains of her dress on the edge. She took Duncan's gun and her holster belt and put both on top of her dress.

Feeling foolish and humiliated, she crawled into the shower. As the steam poured down on her, she let out a moan. It had been weeks since she showered, but the functional design looked foreign compared the heated pools of Kraken's cavern. The shower was short for Eliza, but tall for Billie. She had to kneel in the middle to enjoy it, but it was pure bliss to have the mud cleaned off her body.

Much later, she crawled out and into the sleeping nest. Water dripped from her body and soaked into the cushions. A few droplets steamed when they struck the pillow. She rolled over in the cushions, as they were intended to be used in the smaller nests, to dry herself off.

She moaned and stretched out.

"Feel better?"

Eliza looked up at Billie. "Much better."

"Well," said the tiny raptor as she sat down on the edge of the sleeping nest. "We are well on our way. In a few hour, you will be back with Kraken." Her tail snapped back and forth, quivering with every stroke. She tilted her head to look at something.

Sitting up, Eliza followed Billie's gaze. It was the random images on the screen, of little children bouncing around.

"My family. I miss them even though I will see them in a few hour."

Eliza smiled as she saw the image of herself again, a smile on her face and one hand sticking out of the nest.

The next one was the five baby raptors sleeping in a nest. They were all different colors: purple, red, orange, green, and blue. The only thing they had in common were yellow eyes and splotches of yellow on their bellies.

"My sister," Billie said proudly. "We've been through a lot in the last thirty year."

Eliza barely heard her. Instead, she took in the identical splotches of yellow on the belly of the green raptor. It was the same coloration as the swarm of creatures that attacked her. And patterns ran in families. But, for all the conversations, she never thought of the splotches and eyes as a pattern.

Her throat tightened.

With a glance, she saw her holster was empty. A sinking feeling grabbed her heart and tugged down. Her instincts were right. She shifted to her knees and dug her hand into the cushions. She knew the raptor watched her, so she held herself still and stared into Billie's yellow eye.

Finally, Billie broke the silence. "Family is everything to me."

Body tense, Eliza nodded. She knew Billie was toying with her now, but the little raptor showed no sign of it.

"I'm sorry it came to this."

"You wanted Kraken's colors?"

"Ever since we were born. My mother and my mother's mother. We have been playing this game for four generation."

"You got good at hiding your emotions." Eliza felt dead as she stared at the tiny raptor. She never suspected anything until it was too late. For a moment, she felt like one of the pawns, but with multiple masters.

"When you are up against Kraken, we had to be. His line has been master strategist since the beginning of time."

Eliza grunted. It was the same with her. The Midoze legacy had burned through her veins, as did her flaws. She was excellent at shooting and piloting, but now she was sitting across from a homicidal raptor. She swirled her hand through the cushions, trying to find her firearm.

"It is more than just a pattern. It is a sign of respect and ownership. And, to get here, we had to become just like him. A proper legacy instead of what you will give him."

"What is going to happen?" It took all her willpower not to tear apart the nest. Her hand scraped against the cushions, trying to find the weapon.

"My sister will take over the ship. We steal its secret and his pattern. In a generation, we will take over the nest ship."

"And..." Her voice died as she caught the muzzle of her gun. Flipping it over, she realized she had slowed down her speech. "... the eggs?"

Billie's head lowered. "They are not one of us."

Eliza gulped. "And me?"

"I'm sorry, Eliza. I and all my child like you, but we cannot lose track of our goal." Billie rose up. "Though, my sister's attack on you was not planned, we cannot let you tell Kraken."

She flipped the weapon and held it in her palm.

"We will make it quick, Eliza, I promise." Billie's tail pressed against the cushion. "As quick as we can make it."

"We?"

"My child and my sister. There are a thousand of us, we are docking with the nest ship in a few minute."

"Torn apart by a thousand raptors? That is quick?"

Billie bobbed her head. "There are a thousand of us. You will not suffer long. Sorry," she said but Eliza didn't believe her.

Eliza jerked her hand up, gun in hand.

Billie let out a trill and jumped back. Her body shot across the room.

Eliza pulled the trigger.

The tiny raptor exploded into a shower of burning blood.

Panting, Eliza let out her breath. "Sorry, Billie," but she didn't mean it either.

Scrambling to her feet, she grabbed her holster and raced out of the room. She managed to get it over her hip, the weapon bumping against her thigh. Reaching the cockpit, she threw herself into the seat and began to slap buttons. Billie's lessons on flying the ship came easily to her, and she knew enough of the language to take control.

The display came up, showing a second ship coming close to dock-ing. A countdown flashed over the screen as the automated system took over.

Eliza swore underneath her breath. She started to work her way through the menus, but she spotted an abort button on the dash. Slapping it, she aborted the docking process and swung the ship around.

Billie's ship was far bigger than the fighters Eliza flew. It moved and turned considerably slower, but in space, there was little friction as the massive ship circled around.

As it did, Eliza puzzled through the menus to find the weapons control. Unlike her fighter, which had the weapons as the primary control, the freighter had the system under three layers of menus, buried under a "Utilities" function.

She brought the ship in a straight flight toward the other one. She imagined a thousand snarling raptors waiting to kill her inside.

There was no hesitation when she slapped the control and fired the plasma cannon. There was a blast of plasma and a large hole appeared in the cockpit of the approaching craft. Air burst out the other direction, sucking tiny bodies out of the gaping hole.

Eliza felt dead as she watched them claw at their throats and bel-lies, trying to survive. Tightening her grip on the flight stick, she flew away and let the thousand young die.

She felt a tear burning in her eye as the darkness filled the screen. She liked Billie and her young. They were nice to her and made her dresses. Billie spent hours teaching Eliza how to speak and read the language. And it all ended because of some goal that drove them to kill.

Sniffing, Eliza brought up the display again. She needed to go back to the nest ship. She could see the ship in front of her, it had the symbol for sister over it. There were three more of Billie's family approaching from the fleet ship. The flashing symbols and colors identified them as Billie's other sisters.

Using her finger, Eliza mapped out their destination. It was an un-marked ship on the display, unmoving and without symbol or iden-tification. Without a doubt, she knew it was Kraken's.

Twisting the ship around, she aimed Billie's craft toward it. The eggs weren't safe anymore. The only thing she could do was take them directly to Kraken.

She only had twenty minutes to figure out how.

26 Desperation

By the time the ship docked to Kraken's nest ship, Eliza wished she had a better plan than the one she came up with. As the ship approached, she combed through Billie's ship looking for anything she could use. She found nothing useful except a strip of plastic wrap used for cooking.

And she didn't have long before the raptor ships came.

Her heart beat against her ribs as she waited for the pressure door to open. In her mind, she already had her route planned. Grab the large bucket from the maintenance closet, scoop up the eggs and put them in the bucket, and seal it over. She could set Billie's system to keep the eggs at the right temperature, but a thin plastic shield against the eggs was too risky. She just didn't have another choice.

She rushed inside. The bucket was easy. Her bare feet slipped against the floor as she raced into the pool room. Scooping up the bucket, she set it aside and dove into the muck.

It was comforting and thick, but difficult to swim through. The stuff at the bottom felt like thickened putty. It dragged at her limbs. She felt around the blindly, her fingers scraping against the smooth bottom, but she couldn't find the eggs.

When her lungs began to burn, she turned and pushed up. Her foot caught one of the eggs, but she couldn't grab it before the black spots swam across her vision. Struggling with every movement, she clawed up through the muck.

Her face broke the surface, and she sobbed for air. Panting, she took a deep breath and dove again, heedless of the ache in her lungs and the burning along her limbs. She reached the bottom and grabbed for the eggs. Her fingers found nothing.

The second time she surfaced, she took longer to gasp. She felt the muck pouring down her face and choking her. It burned at the back of her limbs. She didn't know if she could last, but the overwhelming drive to save the eggs forced her back down.

On the fourth attempt, she got lucky and found the curve that drew the eggs to the center of the pool. Her questing fingers caught both of them and she gripped them before kicking up. This time, she didn't have to hesitate stepping down and used that to forced herself up into the air.

She gasped for air, but couldn't wipe her face. Not without bringing the eggs into the oxygen. Gasping and choking on the muck, she swam blindly for the edge and then followed it toward the shallow end of the pool.

Eliza used the edge of the pool to scrape the muck from her face. The textured edge scraped her eyelids, but she could clear her vision enough to find her bucket. Panting, she inched toward it. Her bare feet slipped on the smooth bottom of the pool as she drew closer.

At the bucket, she found a flaw in her plan. Her hands were full and the eggs were too large for one hand. She swore for a minute, then reached up to grab the bucket edge with her mouth and drag it. It was heavy, filled with the chemical slurry around her. Her teeth and neck ached, but she managed to tip it over and drag it into the pool with her.

She gasped for breath, terrified to hear another ship docking with the nest ship. Carefully, she refilled the bucket and placed the two eggs inside. Her body trembled as she set it outside the pool and crawled out.

It took her precious minutes to wrap the bucket in the plastic. She emptied out the entire roll, bringing the wrap up and over the bucket, creating as many layers as she could to protect her eggs.

When she ran out of plastic, she picked up the bucket with both hands and returned to the ship. She placed the bucket in Billie's room, nestled deep in the cushions and then returned to the cockpit.

The display showed the three raptor ships approaching quickly. The massive crafts had been accelerating the entire time, and they would be on her in a second. And Eliza had no doubt they would be armed with at least one plasma cannon each.

She threw herself into the seat and jammed the accelerator. Warnings flashed by, but she canceled them as fast as she saw them. The ship roared and vibrated.

With a screech of metal, her ship tore out of the docking collar. Air burst out of the dock for a few seconds before the pressure door closed.

Eliza only hoped Kraken would forgive her.

27 Dog Fight

An hour later, she was almost upon the asteroid. Behind her, the three raptor ships were matching her speed, but they were out of range for their weapons. Her only saving grace is that her angle from Kraken's nest ship was different than theirs and they had to turn their unwieldy freighters to chase after her.

Eliza sat back down on her chair after checking on the eggs. She panted as she struggled to control herself. They were coming into FCM territory, and she didn't have the access codes or authorization to approach. She was dead, as far as they were concerned.

She considered calling in a mayday, but it felt wrong with her already abandoning the FCM. They were not her family, and the asteroid was not her home. They would sooner shoot her than let her in. And if Ritan got in charge of the orders, they would execute her as fast as they could.

Eliza settled into place and strapped herself in. She knew Billie's ship better now, the weapon systems had been reassigned to one of the buttons. The cannon was slow, but powerful, much like the ship itself. She could see why the FCM had trouble fighting them; while the FCM craft were faster, they had lighter armor. The raptor ships were heavily armored and could easily take dozens of strikes before rupturing.

She closed her eyes and took a deep breath.

On the screen, the threshold of communication from the FCM approached. It was a field of green that indicated the proper distance to hail. It was also the point where the asteroid considered everything within part of the asteroid itself.

She blew past it without touching the communicator.

Almost instantly, the flight coordinator AI sent a hail. "Fleet Freighter Billie 201, you are not authorized for approach. Identify your purpose."

Eliza smirked at the need to have a generation. She guessed that someone had to pick a number, so they choose one higher than the number of generations expected to live and die on the asteroid before it reached its destination.

"Fleet Freighter Billie 201, identify your purpose."

It took Eliza three tries to turn on the communication, not from misunderstanding the menus but from her nervousness. "This is Cap... Eliza Midoze 73, I have an emergency for Fleet Master Kraken."

"Captain Eliza Midoze 73, you are not authorized..." There was a long hiss.

Eliza continued to accelerate the ship. "This is Eliza Midoze 73, I have an emergency packet for Fleet Master Kraken. Please advise him."

"You are not authorized."

"Just let him know!"

"You are not authorized."

Furious, Eliza disconnected the communications. She sighed; it was going to get messy.

Behind her, the three raptor ships entered the FCM communication range. No doubt, they would be hissing a lie. If Eliza guessed right, it would take twenty-two minutes for the fighter pilots to be suited up and launched. She knew the protocols, eight ships in the first round and sixteen in the next. Depending on what was said, they would either be all coming for her or spread out among the four ships.

Her breasts rose and fell as she flipped through the programming of the weapon systems. She tweaked the energy driver for the plasma cannon, increasing the firing time but lowering the power. It would give her more chances to lay down shots that matched more with the fighter pilot's superior weaponry.

She also brought up the landing jets. Normally, the low power rockets were used only to maneuver the ship on a landing bay, but in space, they could give her a chance to move the ship around more gracefully. However, they had limited fuel and she wouldn't be able to land the ship without crashing if she did.

Eliza struggled with the decision, but then prepared the rockets.

"Fleet Freighter Billie 201, you are not authorized for approach. Turn around or the FCM will defend itself."

"This is Eliza Midoze 73, I have an emergency package for Fleet Master Kraken. Just let him know!"

The display wavered for a moment, then Ritan's face loomed over her. "Eliza Midoze 73!"

She glared up at him, still thumping buttons as she struggled to increase her advantage over the FCM fighters. "Colonel."

"Why are you still alive?"

"Because over there, it was self-defense, not murder."

"You killed—"

"And I just killed a thousand more, but that doesn't make it any less defending me from someone trying to kill me."

"I will not—"

"Colonel!"

Ritan jerked, his mouth opened.

"I have an emergency package for Fleet Master Kraken. Please bring him to the comm."

His eyes flickered down and the furrows in his brow deepened. "You're disgusting, Midoze 73. You have no pride or respect for everything we've done for you."

"I have no pride for a place that considered me a flawed genetic mistake."

"You are. If your brother—"

"Duncan is dead."

"You murdered him?"

"He attacked me, and I defended myself. I was happy to remain on the fleet and away from the asteroid, but you sent my brother to kill me."

"Your brother's orders were not to assassinate you."

"What were they?"

Muscles in the colonel's jaw jump. "That is classified."

"And so is my package. By protocol, you are recording this. I have an emergency package for Fleet Master Kraken and must deliver it. Will you give me authorization to land and deliver?"

"No." And the screen went dark.

A klaxon ripped through the darkness. She looked up to see eight fighter craft shooting out of the launch bays of the asteroid. No doubt, there would be at least one of the Midoze, desperate to save the reputation of their genetics, but the rest of them would be far worse pilots than Eliza. It only took her a second to identify which one by the speed and steadiness.

Behind her, the three raptor ships were finally closing in on her.

On screen, the twelve ships sailed toward each other with stately grace. It was not the emotions that Eliza felt as she stared at them. There was a good chance she was going to die in less than an hour and there was nothing she could do about it.

She considered crawling into the nest with the eggs, to hold them as the ship was destroyed, but she had gone too far to give up.

The FCM fighters reached her first. The four cannons of each fighter flashed, but Eliza ignored them. They weren't in range yet. She brought up a hodgepodge of video feeds and display overlays. It was a hacked up system, but she thought it was enough to keep her safer in the battle.

The millisecond her own cannon came in range, she fired at the other Midoze. The plasma streaked across the darkness and exploded into the muzzle of one of the fighters just as it was firing itself. The dual blast of plasma ignited in a fireball which blew the ship into a tailspin away.

Eliza felt only a minute guilt at killing one of her own genetics, but then it faded. In their eyes, she was just as flawed as Ritan claimed.

She fired the docking rockets and spun the ship. The heavy craft continued to sail toward the approaching fighters, but she presented the armored side of her ship to the belch of plasma cannons.

Warning lights and klaxon screamed out as she felt the strikes pummel the ship. Her inertia slowed with every impact, the tiny explosions draining precious movement.

Slowly, the freighter came around just as the fighters peeled away from her. She fired as fast as she could, a single shot belching out. It missed the engine she was aiming for, but sparks flew out from the score that traced a black line the entire length of the smaller fighter.

She continued to turn the ship around until she sailed backwards toward the asteroid. The cannon recharged and she twisted her own ship and fired again, taking out the engine with a well-placed shot.

The other three raptor ships joined into the fray. They fired their own cannons in rapid succession. They missed at first, but Eliza knew that it was only a matter of time before they got lucky.

Shoving the control down, Eliza brought the nose of the ship down and fired the main engines. With a groan, the G-forces pinned her in her chair as the ship strained to change directions without a thousand tons of force twisting it apart.

Plasma blasts and missiles slammed into the top of the ship. The impacts slammed her around in her seat, and she prayed the eggs would be okay.

Her freighter accelerated down and around the asteroid. She panted from the effort and brought the large ship around to fire two more shots, both missing.

Half of the fighters were chasing her now, but the other half were attacking the other raptor ships. She spotted the remains of a fighter exploding as it spun off away from the fight; one of the raptors must have struck it.

Grimly, she brought her freighter around to protect her engines from the fighter's blasts. Her maneuver also aimed her ship directly at the asteroid.

Eliza stared at the massive rock spinning in space. The surface had deep mountains and ridges, along with valleys filled with sharp rocks. The outer skin of her previous home also had airlocks dotting the surface though each one was locked and armored against attack.

Missiles slammed into her ship, knocking it to the side. Smoke drifted through the air, telling her that the damage was getting serious. She couldn't understand the warning displays on the screen, so she swept them aside.

Firing the rockets at full blast, she aimed the freighter for the surface of the asteroid. As soon as she gained enough momentum, she used the rapidly diminishing landing rockets to orient herself parallel to the surface and then fired the main engines.

The freighter blasted forward toward the mountains.

Behind her, missiles and plasma impacted with the side of the asteroid. A second later, the firing stopped. She grinned when she realized why. The AI was conservative and shooting at one's home was not the safest thing to do. They would only take a shot if they were locked on, which gave her a larger margin of survival.

Eliza scanned the surface ahead. She spotted an airlock sailing past her. As it did, she remembered Ritan had given her authorization to enter one. It may be from the wrong direction, but she was sure she could.

Panting with exhilaration, she maneuvered the ship completely and around prepared for a rapid slowdown using the main engines.

As the next airlock came into view, she fired her engines at full. At the same time, she switched over to the maneuvering rockets and brought the freighter down to the airlock.

She had to twitch between the controls rapidly, adjusting the main rocket to reduce her movement to match the asteroid and the maneuvering thrusters to bring her ship near the docking collar. She was sure they would prevent her from docking, but the emergency systems weren't controlled by an AI. It did, however, require the brackets to touch for the automated clamps to activate.

The freighter shuddered from an impact. The fighters had slowed down to almost a stop and were using her lack of movement to aim safely.

Klaxons blared out as they fired their missiles.

Trusting the armor to hold for a few more seconds, she brought the ship to a complete stop and let inertia carry it the last few meters into the docking collar. The ship shuddered when the automated system clamped down.

Fumbling with her restraints, Eliza tore them off her body and sprinted down the hall. Her bare feet slapped loudly and her gun smacked her side as she reached Billie's sleeping nest.

The eggs were on their side. Muck leaked out in a slow trickle into the cushions.

"No!" she screamed. She threw herself into the nest, splashing the muck everywhere. She planted her feet on either side and righted the bucket. The muck inside slopped around.

Panting, she rolled it around in fear that the eggs were exposed to the air. She felt the gentle thunk of the eggs, but she didn't see even a hint of shell. She let out her breath and then a sob.

An attack struck the ship and she was thrown to her knees. She clutched the bucket as the ship rolled. Lifting her foot, she braced it against the side of the nest and forced herself out of the cushions.

The bucket was heavy, but adrenaline poured through her system. She carried it down the corridor to the airlock. More missiles struck the ship and klaxons ripped through the air. Wind rushed toward the cockpit, accelerating with every passing second.

Seeing a hull breach drove her to move faster. With a scream, she reached the airlock and threw herself into it. Her back scraped along the door.

Dropping the bucket in the middle, she spun around and slapped the cycle button.

From somewhere else in the ship, the cockpit she assumed, there was a crunch followed by a bang. The air rushing out became a hurricane that tore out hunks of the wall. Knickknacks and Billie's personal things flew across the airlock opening until the pressure door slammed shut.

Panting, Eliza padded to the opposite side. The sensors indicated a good seal and air. She tapped the release button and the pressure door opened. She dragged the bucket to the door, but then stopped sharply when she realized the asteroid's pressure door had not opened.

A growl ripped out of her. "Open up!"

"Authorization code required." It was the AI.

"Let me in! This is an emergency!"

"Authorization code required."

"This is Eliza, let me in!"

"Authorization code required."

"Damn it, this is Captain Eliza Midoze 73! Let me in!"

There was a beep. "Authorization code accepted. One-time access granted by Master Colonel Ritan."

Eliza let out a sob. The code was good, and she wouldn't die in the hard vacuum of space. Not wanting to experience a missile strike, she grabbed the bucket and dragged it into the airlock.

Behind her, the ship shuddered, and there was an explosion. A heartbeat later, air rushed past her as it was drawn out by a hole rupturing the side of the ship.

She panted as she carried the bucket further into her former home. She was naked, covered in mud, and just tried to kill the very people she trained with. There was no way they would ever let her live.

The pressure door closed with a solid thud.

On the far side, Billie's ship exploded into flames.

Eliza took a deep breath and let it out as a sob. She sank to her knees, crouched over the bucket. She made it.

The whine of an energy weapon halted her joy. Turning around, she saw she was in a cross-junction. Down two of the corridors were four soldiers, two each. Each one held a large energy rifle ready and charged. The soldiers were wearing heavy armor, designed for defense of the asteroid against breeches. Their weapons were capable of firing thousands of times, as long as they were within the wireless charging capabilities of the asteroid.

Against a naked woman, it was overkill.

"Captain Eliza Midoze 73, freeze!" She didn't know which of the four spoke with a harsh metallic voice, but it didn't matter.

She did, but remained crouched over the bucket.

"Remove your weapon by the belt and toss it aside."

Trembling, she unbuckled her weapon holster and lifted it slowly into the air. She tossed it down the third corridor, away from the other soldiers.

"Stand away from the device."

"No."

"Stand away!"

"I have an emergency package for Fleet Master Krak—"

"Stand away!" A single plasma shot burst against the wall. The heat washed over her.

She closed her eyes and screamed. "I have an emergency delivery for Fleet Master Kraken! Let me give it to him!"

"Fleet," came a painfully familiar voice, "Master Kraken will not be coming." She turned to see Ritan gasping as he slumped against the wall. His face was pale with sweat pouring down the sides of his face. He had been running, probably more than he had in many years.

Part of her wanted to smile, but she didn't. "Colonel Ritan, just let—"

"That's Master Colonel Ritan 69 to you!"

"Master Colonel Ritan 69, I must deliver this to Fleet Master Kraken. It is critical and an emergency."

"What is it?" Ritan pushed himself off the wall and staggered down the hall. Behind him, six soldiers lined up with their pulse rifles ready. The muzzles were unwavering and each one hummed with the charge that crackled along the length.

She stared at him for a moment before she shook her head.

"If you don't hand over that..." He looked at it for a moment. "Is that plastic wrap?"

Eliza nodded.

"That came from the egg ship, didn't it?"

She clutched the bucket tightly.

Ritan approached within three meters and stopped. He straightened and made a show of straightening his uniform. "No, I can't let you take it to him."

"Why not?" Her scream echoed shrilly down the corridor.

"Because, he is a threat. He is a danger to our safety and our way of life."

"He's going to leave! They are jumping."

Ritan's face purpled, and he ground his jaw together. "No, he isn't. The fleet isn't going anywhere."

Eliza tensed. "You're going to kill him?"

He said nothing.

"No," she sobbed, "you can't."

"Yes, Captain, I can. And I will." He turned to the soldiers behind him. "Remove those eggs and destroy them."

"No!" screamed Eliza. She clutched the bucket tighter to her body, crushing her breasts and thighs against the sharp edges.

Relief came when an aide rushed up. "Colonel! We have a problem."

Ritan glared at the younger woman. "I'm dealing with it."

"No, the raptors are coming this way!"

Ritan spun on the aide. "I told you to keep them in the meeting hall!"

"I tried, but they slipped out. They are coming this way."

"How? What did you tell them!" He grabbed the aide by her uniform and dragged her closer. "What?"

The aide shuddered before her jaw tightened and her resolve returned. "Nothing, Master Colonel Ritan. The Hissa thought she smelled something and just ran out, the others are following."

Eliza got an idea. She looked down at the black mud on her hand and the muck in the bucket. Kraken would know the smell and Hissa could find her. She bit down on the side of her hand and bit down as hard as she could. Pain exploded along her senses, but she continued to grind down until she thought her jaw would crack.

Releasing it, she stared at her hand. Blood welled up from the perfect indention in her hand. With her other, she wormed her hand into the wraps of plastic to coat her hand. Bringing her two hands together, she mixed the blood and muck together.

Turning around, she took a deep breath and forced herself to calm down. It wasn't a weapon, but she imagined herself shooting once again. Her left hand trembled, but her right grew steady.

She coated the end of her finger with the muck and blood. Crouching over the bucket, she aimed for the aide and flicked.

The splatter arched into the air and splattered a meter short of her target.

Ritan was still screaming at the aide, but she didn't hear the words.

She gathered up another glob and flicked it. It fell short again.

"Captain Midoze 73!" One of the soldiers snapped out. "Cease moving!"

Eliza froze, waiting for the plasma blast.

Ritan spun around. "Stand up, Eliza."

"No!"

"Stand up or I will have you shot where you are."

Eliza shook her head, then looked at the blood welling in her hand. She gulped and realized she had one last chance to mark the aide.

She made a show of nodding. Rubbing her hands together, she gathered up as much as she could and slowly stood up. Her heartbeat slowed down and her body quieted. She let her breath in a long, slow sigh.

"Now, turn around and face your execution like a... human."

The soldiers braced themselves. The whine of the rifles filled the air.

Eliza nodded and took another breath.

She gathered up as much as she could and turned around sharply. As she did, she flung her hand out. It was almost a graceful gesture as the thick glob of muck and blood shot out from her hand.

One of the soldiers fired and the heat of the plasma burned her breast, face, and arm as it clipped her shoulder.

Eliza staggered, almost dropping to her knees. Her left arm went limp. She screamed out as the pain radiated from her body. She couldn't feel her shoulder, but the red-hot agony tore through her. Shuddering, she looked over to see part of her shoulder had been burned away, leaving a hunk of charred bone and cooked muscles visible through the gap.

Everyone froze. The silence was deafening.

Eliza struggled to keep from screaming. She turned away from the blackened burn and struggled through a wave of exhaustion and agony that clawed at her senses.

Ritan laughed. "Is that it?"

She trembled as she looked at him.

Her attack had splattered Ritan across his face but completely missed the aide. She groaned; she missed.

Ritan wiped his face on his sleeve. Then, he looked at the muck and groaned. "You ruined my uniform, Captain. At least you can take that to your death."

Eliza spat at him; it missed by meters.

He turned around. "Execute her and destroy the bucket."

Rifles hummed loudly.

One of the soldier called out. "On three. Three!"

Eliza straightened herself and pushed the bucket behind her, as if she could stop a plasma blast from even one of the rifles.

"Two!"

A roar ripped through the corridor, echoing painfully against the perfectly smooth walls.

Two of the soldiers faltered, but the others remained in position. "One!"

Eliza cringed.

A thud shook through the corridor. Heavy footsteps slammed into the ground. Eliza looked up to see Hissa charging down the corridor. The red raptor punched through the soldiers, tossing them aside. Her claws tore through the floor and her eyes were fixed forward.

"Fire!"

Plasma exploded around Eliza. She screamed out as it burned her, ripping at her nerves and choking her.

Hissa's body slammed into her, slamming her back against the airlock.

The impact drove the air out of her lungs. Eliza's head slammed against the bulkhead and sparks exploded across her vision.

She fell from the wall and slumped over the smoldering corpse of Hissa. The plasma and smoke rose around her, acidic and choking. She clutched at the raptor and tried not to see the gaping holes in her side or the charred remains of her chest.

Eliza gasped. "No!"

Ritan's voice snapped out as the scream died in her throat. "Fire again."

A roar filled the corridor. It was deep and rumbling, a sound that brought Eliza to her knees. It was Kraken.

She sobbed as she looked up.

The massive raptor thudded down the corridor, his head low and his tail almost flat against the ground. His body shook with anger and drool dribbled out of the side of his mouth. "If you," he growled, "shoot, then you will have war."

Ritan spun around. "Keep out of this! This is FCM business."

The soldiers nearest to Kraken and Ritan turned, bringing their rifles to bear on the raptor passing them.

Kraken snarled and gestured at Eliza with his chin. "That raptor is not FCM. That item is not FCM. That human is not FCM. This is not a FCM matter."

"She's attacked our ships. She is the enemy, a traitor!"

Kraken turned as he passed Ritan, putting his body between Eliza and Ritan. "Really."

"Yes! She had orders—"

"She is not FCM!" roared Kraken.

"She will be executed! Soldier! F—"

Kraken roared. "If you fire, there will be war!"

Eliza tensed, but no plasma shots rang out.

No one spoke, but Eliza couldn't hear anything over the pounding in her ears. She gasped and pushed the bucket away from Hissa, afraid of the heat damaging the eggs.

Kraken's growl shook the air, a wave of noise that rose and fell with every pant.

Ritan, his face still purple, snarled as he stared back at the Kraken.

Eliza gulped and inhaled. "I have an emergency delivery for Fleet Master Kraken. I have said nothing else since I entered communications range." It was simple words, but one spoken into a silent corridor.

Kraken turned to look at her.

She nodded and pushed the bucket further away from Hissa.

The raptor turned back. "Is this true?"

Ritan sputtered. "Of course... no! She did not!"

"Really," came the low growl.

Eliza shook her head. "Yes, I did."

Kraken's tail thumped against the ground.

"Attention on deck! Admiral of the Ship!"

Eliza started to salute, but her hand wouldn't move. She slumped back and looked down the corridor for the admiral.

And then she saw him. An old man in a mechanical wheelchair rolling with twelve elite soldiers flanking him. Behind him, Gornak walked with a steady pace, the raptor's head bobbing.

Ritan paled and stepped back to salute.

Kraken bowed his head.

Eliza followed suit, it was as good of a salute as she could without being a member of the FCM.

"What is going on?" asked the admiral.

Eliza answered. "I have an emergency package for Fleet Master—"

"Stop saying that!" snapped Ritan.

The admiral raised his hand. "Colonel, be quiet." He looked at Eliza but didn't approach. "You've been saying that from the beginning?"

"Y-yes, Admiral."

The admiral looked up. "Quantor?"

"Yes, Admiral of the Ship?" It was a voice that Eliza had never heard before, the master AI for the entire asteroid.

"Display any recordings."

"Recordings have been sealed under emergency order 240019."

"Dismissed."

Ritan slumped against the wall, his face white.

A display over Eliza flashed to life. It played back her frantic call to Ritan. She looked up to watch, dizzy as she saw a woman covered in muck and desperate screaming back.

Kraken stepped over Hissa. His head lowered to Eliza until his nose pressed against her cheek.

She sobbed and looked away from the display. She clutched his head and pressed her cheek harder against his face. "I'm sorry. Duncan came for me with Billie, I think. They both tried to kill me, and Billie's sisters were coming. And I had to keep the eggs safe. And I didn't know what to do. And... and..." She was babbling but didn't care.

"A good move," he rumbled.

The admiral cleared his throat. "I've seen enough. Colonel, I'm disappointed with you."

The playback stopped.

Ritan opened his mouth and then closed it.

Kraken straightened up. "Admiral?"

"Yes, Fleet Master Kraken?"

The raptor stepped away from Eliza and Hissa. His claws thudded against the ground, but his tail slithered around to hold Eliza. "I suspect one of my own has betrayed the fleet while working with him. May I confirm?"

"Yes, of course."

Kraken looked up, mimicking the admiral. "Um, Quantor?"

"Ready, Fleet Master Kraken."

"Were there any communications between Colonel Ritan and Billie of the Fleet?" No one seemed to notice Kraken pronouncing Ritan's name correctly.

"No such entity exists."

Eliza saw Ritan smirk for a moment. She cleared her throat. She looked down at Hissa and fought her anger. There was something, but Ritan had hidden it. She remembered the response from the AI as she approached. Clearing her throat, she said, "Are there any recording between Master Colonel Ritan 69 and Fleet Pilot Billie 201?"

Ritan's face dropped again.

"There are three such recordings."

Eliza sighed. "There always has to be a generation."

The admiral waved his hand. "The last one, please."

The display flashed with Billie up on front. "Do we have a deal?"

Off-screen, Ritan spoke. "Most do not start conversations in this manner. Nor without warning me. I need to seal these records before you call and prevent the recordings. It takes time."

"I am impatient and I will be fast. Kraken just took Eliza to the egg ship. I do not have much time before the eggs are hatched. We cannot afford to let another Kraken take reins of the fleet ship. Do we have a deal?"

Ritan sighed. "Yes, I will send my best man."

The little raptor bobbed her head. She was in her ship cockpit, and her tail quivered with her excitement. "Good, good. You get my family the egg ship and we give you half the heavy fighter in the fleet and jump. Kraken can have his accident on your ship."

"And plans for all the technologies in the fleet?"

"Of course. When my family is Kraken, then you get everything." Her body shook with excitement.

Kraken snorted as the display ended. "Half the heavy fighter? You do not have facilities for a thousand ships."

Ritan stared at him. "A-A thousand? But, in the fight, you only had twenty."

Kraken turned on him, staring at him with one bright blue eye. "We are raptor. We do not fight duel and we do not fight with honor, we swarm. Not one, not a hundred. When we fight for blood, every-one fight. And, if you wish to see what two thousand heavy fighter, five thousand light, and a thousand long-range launcher look like. Wait two hour. If you wish to see what a million strong raptor look like in your corridor, wait two more and follow the scream." His voice with a low snarl as he stated it as a fact, not a threat.

Ritan sputtered, but the admiral cut him off. "Why?"

Kraken turned to the senior officer. "When I smelled my mate on board with my egg, I ordered a mobilization. I will kill for both."

Eliza smiled at Kraken's use of "mate" and then hid it before any-one else noticed.

The admiral cleared his throat. "Fleet Master Kraken, I think we need to talk."

Kraken smiled. "Yes, but my mate and my egg come first. That will give you time to deal with your," he turned toward Ritan, "sub-ordinate. And decide how you want to handle the revelation." His tail shook with a quiver of excitement. "And remember the demand you gave on me for the death of your two liaison. An exchange, a life for life."

He turned toward Eliza, drawing her close. "And if my mate or my egg is harmed, there will be no more FCM left when your asteroid reach its home. Do you understand?" He looked over his shoulder at the admiral.

His own face growing red, the Admiral of the Ship nodded.

Kraken turned toward Eliza, his tail shaking. He reached out with his head.

Eliza lifted her chin to meet him, panting softly as he pressed his nose against her cheek.

"Unexpected, but you made a very good move."

28 Epilogue

Eliza of the Raptors stood on the landing platform of the nest ship. The wind whipped around her, cutting at her nearly naked skin. Her dress fluttered along her thighs, tickling her skin as the wind tugged at the yellow fabric.

In front of her, the former FCM fighter ship stood nestled in its cradle. The black paint had been replaced in her colors, yellow with red stripes. It was one of the many things Kraken took from the FCM as part of the deal to avoid a slaughter.

"Mama?" Claws dug at her shin.

She looked down at the raptor at her side. Her red skin was the color of blood, and the yellow stripes were almost identical to Kraken's. The only different was the smallest hint of yellow at the tip of her nose and along her toes. With a smile, she reached down and scooped up the little raptor. "Good morning, Kiki, did you have a good nap?"

"Yes, Mama." The little raptor pointed to the ship. "Is that your ship? It has your colors." Growing up with two languages, Kiki managed to grasp plurals where most of the other raptors didn't.

"Yes, it is."

"Will you take fly with me?" The raptor's voice was high-pitched but vibrated with her purr.

"Yes," Eliza kissed her on the nose. "I will. But, after the jump. Right now, you need to go with Corsair and return to the nest."

Kraken's footsteps thudded on the ground as he approach. Around his feet, Kiki's brother hopped from claw to claw, trilling with his amusement.

"Yes," growled Kraken. "Time to return to the nest."

"I love you, Mama!" trilled Kiki.

"Me too, Mama!" called Corsair.

Gornak bobbed his head and barked twice. The two baby raptors raced after him.

Eliza smiled and turned from her ship. Kraken's end move had been magnificent, a culmination of observation and maneuverings that gave almost all FCM technology to the fleet along with a sizable donation of weapons, supplies, and crew. The humans, all of them desperate to leave the rigid world of the FCM, joined willingly and were already dispersing among the many living caverns and groupings.

Kraken nuzzled against Eliza's cheek. "You smell nice."

She leaned into him. "So do you..." She sniffed. A heady musk filled the air. Her breath quickened as she trailed her eyes down his body to where his cock was already emerging from its sheath.

Her pussy clenched with anticipation. "Aren't you suppose to hunt me before that happened?"

He nipped at her ear. "I've been chasing you since the day I saw you. I just finally caught you."

A heat washed over her, spreading out from her body. With a grin, she kissed him and then sprinted away.

About t'Sade...

t'Sade has been happily using third-person singular since the late eighties. Besides that strange quirk, they enjoy writing a brutal combination of sex and violence for decades. Most of their stories explore the fringe edges of sexuality in the epic quest of trying to write a story for every fetish and turn-on known to the human libido.

It's going to take a long time.

They have over a hundred stories for free on their websites. The darker stuff can be found at tsade.com and the lighter stories can be found under their alternate name, D. Sadie, which can be found at dsadie.com.

Also by t'Sade

All of these novels can be found at Curious Cabbit Press (curiouscabbit.com) and are available at many print and ebook sites.

The Mummy's Girl

In a love story spanning centuries, The Mummy's Girl is an epic, erotic tale set in a land of pure fantasy. A cruel master with a warm heart punishes a new slave in the temple of a wolf-god, discovering that it is more for her pleasure than her pain, and gradually finds himself falling in love with her. They are not destined to be together when death by betrayal tears them apart. One sacrifices her soul to bring her master to life, cursing him to walk the earth as a mummy, a creature of death, sex, and magic. But, even as they are torn apart, the games of gods scheme to reunite the star-crossed lovers.

Many variations of fantastic BDSM and sexuality blend together in the twisting reincarnations of two souls as they seek each other. When they finally become one, it is only through divine submission and sacrifice of mind and boy that gives them that final chance to be reunited.

Colophon

This edition was written using Emacs and formatted using Markdown. It was then translated into DocBook 5 XML before being transformed into PDF via XeLaTeX.

The font used is SIL's Gentium Book Basic.

The front cover was illustrated by Mamabliss and typeset in Solomon Sans. More of their work can be found at http://mamabliss.com/.

www.ingramcontent.com/pod-product-compliance
Lightning Source LLC
Chambersburg PA
CBHW020431180626
46812CB00003B/1181